Lie
With
Me

— A Novel —

PHILIPPE BESSON

Translated from the French by
Molly Ringwald

SCRIBNER
New York   London   Toronto   Sydney   New Delhi

Scribner
An Imprint of Simon & Schuster, Inc.
1230 Avenue of the Americas
New York, NY 10020

First Scribner hardcover edition April 2019

SCRIBNER and design are registered trademarks of The Gale Group, Inc., used under license by Simon & Schuster, Inc., the publisher of this work.

For information about special discounts for bulk purchases, please contact Simon & Schuster Special Sales at 1-866-506-1949 or business@simonandschuster.com.

The Simon & Schuster Speakers Bureau can bring authors to your live event. For more information or to book an event, contact the Simon & Schuster Speakers Bureau at 1-866-248-3049 or visit our website at www.simonspeakers.com.

Interior design by Jill Putorti

Manufactured in the United States of America

10 9 8 7 6 5 4

Library of Congress Cataloging-in-Publication Data is available.

ISBN 978-1-5011-9787-1
ISBN 978-1-5011-9789-5 (ebook)

In memory of Thomas Andrieu
(1966–2016)

You didn't have to attract desire. . . . Either it was there at first glance or else it had never been. It was instant knowledge of sexual relationship or it was nothing.

—Marguerite Duras, *The Lover*

I concluded with an aching finality that the could-happen possibilities were gone, and that doing whatever you wanted was over. The future didn't exist anymore. Everything was in the past and would stay there.

—Bret Easton Ellis, *Lunar Park*

One day—I can say precisely when, I know the date—I find myself in the bar of a hotel lobby in a provincial city, sitting in an armchair across from a journalist, a low round table between us, being interviewed for my latest novel, which recently came out. She's questioning me on the themes of the book, on separation, the act of writing letters, whether exile can ever save us. I answer her almost without thinking. I'm used to the questions so the words come easily, almost mechanically, as I allow my gaze to wander to the people walking across the lobby. I watch their comings and goings, and invent the lives of these people in my mind. I try to imagine where they are coming from and where they are headed. I've always loved to do that, to invent the lives of strangers in passing. It could almost be considered an obsession. I believe it started when I was a child. I remember its worrying my mother. "Stop with your lies!" she would say. She used the word "lies" instead of "stories," but nevertheless, it continued, and all these years later, I still find myself doing it. I'm inventing these scenarios in my head while answering questions about the pain of abandoned women—I'm good at that, at disconnecting, at doing these two things at once—when I notice the back of a young man dragging a small rolling suitcase behind him. I stare at this man in the process of leaving the hotel. I know he's young, his youth is emanating from him, in the way he's dressed and in his casual allure. I'm dumbstruck. I think, *This is not possible. This is an image that cannot exist.* I could be mistaken, of course— after all, I don't see his face, I can't see it from where I'm sitting—but still I am absolutely certain I know what the face of this young man looks like. And then I tell myself again, *No, it's impossible—literally impossible*, but still I call out a name. "Thomas!" I actually shout it. "Thomas!" The journalist who's been sitting across from me trying to scribble down everything I've been saying raises her head. Her shoulders tighten, as though it's her I'm shouting at. I know I should apologize, but I don't. I'm too caught up in this image that's now moving away from me, waiting to see if my shouting his name has any effect. He doesn't turn around. The man keeps walking so I should assume that I'm wrong, for sure this time—that it really is just a mirage. That it's just the comings and goings that caused this strange illusion. But instead, I jump up and go after him. It's not so much verification I need, because in the moment I'm still convinced I'm right—right against all reason, against all evidence. I catch up to the man on the pavement just outside the hotel. I put my hand on his shoulder and he turns around.

Chapter One
1984

It's the playground of a high school, an asphalt courtyard surrounded by ancient gray stone buildings with big tall windows. Teenagers with backpacks or schoolbags at their feet stand around chatting in small groups, the girls with the girls and boys with boys. If you look carefully you might spot a supervisor among them, barely older than the rest.

It's winter.

You can see it in the bare branches of a tree you would think was dead planted there in the middle of the courtyard, and in the frost on the windows, and in the steam escaping from mouths and the hands rubbing together for warmth.

It's the mid eighties.

You can tell from the clothes, the high-waisted ultra-skinny acid-wash jeans, the patterned sweaters. Some of the girls wear woolen leggings in different colors that pool around their ankles.

I'm seventeen years old.

I don't know then that one day I won't be seventeen. I don't know that youth doesn't last, that it's only a moment, and then it disappears and by the time you finally realize it, it's too late. It's finished, vanished, lost. There are some around me who can sense it; the adults repeat it constantly but I don't listen. Their words roll over me but don't stick. Like water off the feathers of a duck's back. I'm an idiot. An easygoing idiot.

I'm a student in terminal C at the Lycée Elie Vinet de Barbezieux.

Barbezieux doesn't exist.

Or let's put it another way. No one can say: "I know this place, I can point to it on a map," except perhaps for the readers (and they are more and more rare) of Jacques Chardonne, a Barbezieux native who in his writing extolled the town's implausible "happiness." Or those (and they are more numerous) who have a memory of taking Route 10 to formally begin their vacation at the beginning of August, in Spain or in Les Landes, only to find themselves stuck there—precisely there—in bumper-to-bumper traffic, thanks to a succession of poorly thought-out traffic lights and a narrowing of the highway.

It is in Charente, thirty kilometers south of Angoulême. The limestone soil lends itself to the cultivation of vines, unlike the cold, clay soil of neighboring Limousin. It's an oceanic climate, with mild and rainy winters. There isn't always a summer. As far back as I can remember, it's the gray that dominates, and the humidity. The remains of Gallo-Roman churches, and scattered chateaux. Ours looked like a fortified castle but what was there really to defend? Surrounding us there were hills. It was said the landscape undulated. That's about it.

I was born there. Back then we still had a maternity ward, but it closed many years ago. No one is born in Barbezieux anymore, the town is doomed to disappear.

And who knows Elie Vinet? They claim he was Montaigne's teacher though this fact has never been seriously established. Let's say he was a humanist of the sixteenth century, a translator of Catullus and the principal of the College of Guyenne in Bordeaux. As luck would have it, that brought him to Saint-Médard, an enclave of Barbezieux. The high school was named after him. We didn't find anyone better.

And finally, who remembers the C terminals? They say "S" today, I think. Even if this initial does not represent the same reality. These were the classes in mathematics, supposedly the most selective, the most prestigious. The ones that opened the doors to the preparatory classes that in turn led to the big schools, while the others condemned you to local colleges or professional studies or vocational school or just stopped there, as though you had been left in a cul-de-sac.

So I'm from a bygone era, a dying city, a past without glory.

Understand me, though, I wasn't depressed about it. This was just how it was. I didn't choose it. Like everyone else, I made do.

At seventeen, I don't have a clear awareness of the situation. At seventeen, I don't dream of a modern life somewhere out there, in the stars, I just take what's given to me. I don't nurse any ambition, nor do I carry around any resentment. I'm not even particularly bored.

I am an exemplary student, one who never misses a class, who almost always gets the best grades, who is the pride of his teachers. Today, I'd like to slap this seventeen-year-old kid, not because of the good grades but because of his incessant need to please those who would judge him.

I'm on the playground with everyone else. It's recess. I just got out of two hours of philosophy (*"Can one assume at the same time the liberty of man and the existence of the unconscious?"*), the kind of subject we are told can show up on "the bac," the French end-of-high-school exam. I'm waiting for my biology class. The cold stings my cheeks. I'm wearing a predominantly blue Nordic sweater. A shapeless sweater that I wear too often.

Jeans, white sneakers. And glasses. They're new. My vision deteriorated drastically the year before. I became myopic over the course of a couple of weeks without knowing why and was ordered to wear glasses. I obeyed; I couldn't do otherwise. My hair is fine and curly, my eyes greenish. I'm not beautiful, but I get attention; that I know. Not because of my appearance, but because of my grades. "He is brilliant," they whisper, "much more advanced than the others, he will go far, like his brother, this family is one to be reckoned with." We are in a place, in a moment, where nearly everyone goes nowhere; it garners me equal parts sympathy and antipathy.

I am this young man there, in the winter of Barbezieux.

With me are Nadine A., Genevieve C., Xavier C. Their faces are engraved in my memory when many others, more recent, have deserted me. They aren't the ones I'm interested in though, but rather a boy in the distance leaning against the wall flanked by two other guys around his age. He's a boy with shaggy hair, the hint of a beard, and a serious look. A boy from another class. Terminal D. Another world. There is an impenetrable border that stands between us. Maybe it's contempt. Disdain, at the very least.

But I don't see anyone but him, this slender and distant boy who doesn't speak, who's happy just to listen to the two guys talking next to him without interrupting. Without even smiling.

I know his name. Thomas Andrieu.

I should tell you: I'm the son of the teacher, the school principal. I grew up in a primary school eight kilometers from

Barbezieux, in a first-floor apartment that was assigned to us above the village's only schoolroom. My father was my teacher from kindergarten through middle school. Seven years of receiving his teachings, him in a gray button-down writing on the chalkboard, at the head of the room, us behind our wooden desks. Seven years heated by an oil stove, maps of France covering the walls; maps of an old France, with her rivers and tributaries, and the names of the towns written in a size proportional to their population, published by Armand Colin, and the shadow on the wall of the two linden trees outside the window. Seven years of saying "sir" during school hours, not because he asked it of me, but to make myself indistinguishable from my classmates, and also because my father embodied a quiet authority. After school, I stayed in the classroom with him to do my homework while he prepared the lessons for the following day, tracing in his big checkered notebook, filling the boxes with his beautiful handwriting. He turned on the radio to Jacques Chancel's *Radioscopie*.

I haven't forgotten. I came from this childhood.

My father insisted on good grades. I simply didn't have the right to be mediocre or even average. There was only one place for me—first. He claimed that I would find salvation in my studies, that only study could "allow one to enter the elevator." He wanted the top-ranking higher education establishments for me, nothing else. I obeyed, just as I had with my glasses. I had to.

*   *   *

I recently returned to this place of my childhood, this village that I hadn't set foot in for years. I went back with S. so that he would *know*. The grid was still there with the ancient wisteria, but the lime trees had been cut down, and the school had closed a long time ago. There are housing units there now. I pointed out the window of my room to him. I tried to imagine the new occupants, but I couldn't. After, we took the car out again and I showed him the place where a delivery truck (an old Citroën van that served as a sort of mini-market) came to town every two days, the stable where we would go to get our milk, the decrepit church, the little sloping cemetery, the forest that sprouted mushrooms at the beginning of October. He never imagined I came from such a rural, almost fossilized world. He told me, "It must have taken great will and determination to have lifted yourself out." He didn't say "ambition" or "courage" or "hate." I told him: "It was my father who wanted it for me. I would have stayed in this childhood, in this cocoon."

Thomas Andrieu, I don't know who his father is or even if that matters. I don't know where he lives. At that moment, I don't know anything about him, except for terminal D. And his shaggy hair and somber look.

His name I know because I found it out for myself. Just

like that, one day in the most casual way, before moving on to something else. But I didn't find out any other details.

I absolutely didn't want him to know that I was interested in him, because I didn't want anyone to wonder *why* I was interested in him. Asking that question would only fuel the rumors about me. They say that I "prefer boys." They say that I move like a girl sometimes. I'm not any good at sports, incapable of lifting weights or throwing the javelin, and completely uninterested in soccer and volleyball. Also, I love books, I read all the time. I can often be seen coming out of the school library with a novel in my hands. And I don't have a girlfriend. That's enough to give me a reputation. The insults blend together regularly: "dirty fag" (sometimes just "faggot"), yelled from far away or murmured right next to me. I try to ignore them, to never respond, to manifest a perfect indifference, as though I didn't hear anything (as though it would have been possible not to). But that only makes it worse: a real heterosexual boy would never allow that kind of thing to be said about him. He would vehemently deny it and beat up the person who gave the insult. To allow it to be said is to confirm it.

Of course I "prefer boys."

But I'm not capable of saying this sentence out loud yet.

I discovered my orientation very young, at eleven years old. Even then I knew. My attraction was for a boy in the village who was two years older than me named Sébastien. The house that he lived in, not far from ours, had an addition, a sort of barn. Upstairs, after climbing a makeshift staircase, you would enter a room full of anything and everything. There was even a mattress. It was on this mattress where I rolled around in Sébastien's embrace for the first time. We had not gone through puberty yet, but we were already curious about each other's bodies. His was the first male sex I held in my hand, other than my own. My first kiss was the one he gave me. My first embrace, skin against skin, was with him.

We took refuge in my parents' camper, which was parked in our garage for the winter at the end of the season. (At the beginning of spring it will be found in the Saint-Georges-de-Didonne campground, where we spend weekends walking on the beach, buying churros at the waterfront and fresh shrimp at the market that will end up in bowls later when it's time for drinks before dinner.)

I knew where the key was. It was dark and the air was stale but while the gestures could have been more precise, we were not modest.

Today I'm struck by our creativity because at the time, there was no Internet, not even videocassettes or cable TV. We had never seen any porn, and yet we still knew how to do it. There are things one knows how to do even as a child. By puberty, we would be even more imaginative. That would come fast.

I was not at all troubled by this revelation. On the contrary, it enchanted me. First, because it played out in the dark and children are fond of secret games. And then also because I didn't see the harm in feeling good; I had experienced pleasure with Sébastien and I couldn't conceive of associating that pleasure with anything wrong. Finally because this union crystallized my difference. So I would not resemble the others after all. In this one regard, I would stop being the model child. I wouldn't follow the pack. Out of instinct, I despised packs. That has never changed.

Later I'll hear the famous insults, the obscene insinuations. I'll see the effeminate gestures that are overplayed in my presence, the limp wrists, the rolling eyes, the mimed blow jobs. If I shut up, it's just to avoid being confronted by violence. Is it cowardice? Perhaps. I prefer to see it as a kind of necessary self-protection. But I will never change. I will never think: *It's bad*, or *It would be better to be like everyone else*, or *I will lie to them so that they'll accept me*. Never. I stick to who I am. In silence, of course, but it's a proud, stubborn silence.

I remembered the name. Thomas Andrieu.

I find it a handsome name, a beautiful identity. I don't know yet that one day I will write books, that I will invent characters and I will have to name those characters, but I am already sensitive to the sound of identities, to their fluidity. However, I do know that first names can betray a social origin, a context that anchors those who carry them to a particular era.

I will discover that Thomas Andrieu is ultimately a misleading name.

First of all, Thomas was not a common name given to boys during the sixties in France ("my" Thomas is eighteen years old in 1984). Usually the boys then were named Phillippe, Patrick, Pascal, or Alain. In the seventies, it's the Christophes, Stéphanes, and Laurents that will prevail. The Thomases will make their breakthrough in the nineties. So the black-eyed boy is ahead of his time. Or rather it's his parents who are. That's what I deduce. And then yet again, I will discover that that's not the case either. It was the name of a grandfather who died prematurely, is all.

The Andrieu surname is an enigma. It could be the name of a general, of a man of the cloth, of a farmer. All the same, it strikes me as an everyman's name without my knowing enough to justify that thought.

I can imagine everything. And I don't deprive myself of doing so. On certain days, T.A. is a bohemian child from a family sympathetic to the May '68 riots. On other days, he's the wanton son of a bourgeois couple, as the children of uptight parents often are.

It's my obsession with inventing characters. I told you about this.

In any case, I like to repeat his name to myself in secret. I like to write it on scraps of paper. I am stupidly sentimental: that hasn't changed much.

So, that morning I stand on the playground and secretly stare at Thomas Andrieu.

It's a moment that has occurred before. On many occasions,

I've briefly cast an eye in his direction. It's also happened that I've passed him in the hallway, seen him coming toward me, brushed up against him, felt him receding behind my back without turning around. I've found myself in the lunchroom at the same time, him eating lunch with the guys from his class, me with my friends, but we've never shared the same table; the classes don't mix. One time I spotted him as he stood on the dais during a class, making a presentation. Certain classrooms have windows and this time, I slowed down to study him. He was too busy doing his presentation to notice me. Sometimes he sits alone on the steps in front of the school and smokes a cigarette. I caught his blind gaze once as the smoke evaporated from his mouth. At night, I've seen him leave the school, headed to the Campus, a bar that adjoins the school along the National 10 highway, probably to meet up with friends. Passing in front of the windows of the bar, I recognized him drinking a beer, playing pinball. I remember the movement of his hips pressing against the pinball machine.

But there has never been a word exchanged between us. No contact, not even inadvertently, and I always stopped myself from lingering so as not to arouse his surprise or discomfort at being stared at.

I'm thinking *he doesn't know me at all*. Of course he's probably seen me, but there can be nothing fixed in his memory, not the slightest image. Maybe he's heard the rumors about me, but he doesn't mix with the ones who whistle at and mock me.

There's no chance either that he's heard the praise the teachers have given me: we've never been in the same class.

To him, I'm a stranger.

I'm in this state of one-way desire.

I feel this desire swarming in my belly and running up my spine. But I have to constantly contain and compress it so that it doesn't betray me in front of others. Because I've already understood that desire is visible.

Momentum too; I feel it. I sense a movement, a trajectory, something that will bring me to him.

This feeling of love, it transports me, it makes me happy. At the same time, it consumes me and makes me miserable, the way all impossible loves are miserable.

I am acutely aware of the impossibility.

Difficulty, you can cope with; you can deploy ruses, try to seduce. There is beauty in the hope of conquest. But impossibility, by nature, carries with it a sense of defeat.

This boy is *obviously* not for me.

And not even because I'm not attractive or seductive. It's simply because he's lost to boys. He's not for us, for those *like me*. It's the girls who will win him.

Not only that, all the girls are in his orbit. They circle him, constantly seeking his attention. Even those who feign indifference do so only to win his favor.

And him; he watches what they do. He knows that they find him attractive. Good-looking guys always know it. It's a calm kind of certainty.

Sometimes he lets them approach. I've already seen him with a select few, usually the pretty ones. Immediately I feel a fleeting stab of jealousy, a sense of impotence.

But that being the case, most of the time, he seems to keep the girls at a distance, choosing the company of his guy friends. His preference for friendship, or at least the camaraderie that comes with it, seems to outweigh any other consideration. And I'm surprised, precisely because he could easily use his beauty as a weapon; he is at the age of conquests, when one often impresses others by multiplying those conquests. However his reticence does nothing to feed a secret hope in me. It just makes him even more appealing because I admire those who don't use what they have at their disposal.

He also likes his solitude. It's obvious. He speaks little, smokes alone. He has this attitude, his back up against the wall, looking up toward the sun or down at his sneakers, this manner of not quite being there in the world.

I think I love him for this loneliness, that it's what pushed me toward him. I love his aloofness, his disengagement with the outside world. Such singularity moves me.

But let's come back to that winter morning in 1984. It's a winter of violent winds, bad weather, shipwrecks in the English Channel and snowstorms on the mountains, we see the rush of these images on the morning news. It's a morning that should have been like all the others, consumed by my desire and his ignorance of it. Except on that particular morning, the unexpected happens.

As recess draws to a close and the bell rings, announcing the beginning of class, students leave the biting cold of the playground and go back into the hallways, talking mostly about politics, television shows, and our next vacation, coming in February.

Nadine, Genevieve, and Xavier head off to get their school bags from the student lounge, leaving me alone. I'm crouched down trying to find my biology textbook in the mess of my backpack when suddenly I sense a presence beside me. I immediately recognize the white sneakers. It's excruciating. Slowly, I raise my head to look at the boy above me. Thomas Andrieu is standing there, also alone. He's framed by a cloudless blue sky, cold sun rays behind him. His friends are probably taking the stairs back up to class. Later he will tell me that he invented a pretext for them to go ahead without him, saying he had to pick up a magazine at the library, or something like that. He stands there in the winter cold with me at his feet. I get up, surprised, trying not to betray my confusion and fear. I think he might punch me. The idea crosses my mind that he could beat my face in without a witness. I don't know why he would do such a thing; maybe the insults are no longer enough and he has to do something more concrete. In any case, I tell myself it's in the realm of possibility, that it can happen—which says a lot about the antipathy I believe I provoke, but also my oblivion, because instead he calmly says: I don't want to go to the lunchroom today. We can eat a sandwich in town. I know a place. He gives me an address and an exact time. I look at him for a moment and then say that I'll be there. He briefly closes his eyes, as if in relief. And then he's gone, without saying another word. I remain dumbly rooted to the spot with my biology book in my hand before crouching down again to close my backpack. I know that this scene just happened, I'm not crazy, and at the same time it seems entirely *unbelievable*. I scan the asphalt tarmac, the emptiness of the playground, surrounded by a growing silence.

For a long time I will return to this moment, a moment in which a young man approached me with a confident stride. I think of it as the perfect little crack in an extraordinarily brief window of opportunity.

If I had not been abandoned by my friends, if he had failed to convince his to leave him behind, this moment would not have taken place. It could have almost never happened.

I try to figure out the part that chance played, to assess the nature of the risk that led to the encounter, but I don't succeed. We are in the land of the unthinkable. (Later he will tell me that he waited for the right moment to approach me but until that morning it had never arisen.)

In later years, I will often write about the unthinkable, the element of unpredictability that determines outcomes. And game-changing encounters, the unexpected juxtapositions that can shift the course of a life.

It starts there, in the winter of my seventeenth year.

At the given hour, I push open the door of the café.

It's at the end of the town. I'm surprised by the choice of the place, since it's not at all central, or easily accessible. I think: *He must like places away from the crowd.* I do not yet understand that he obviously chose it to be out of sight. I am in this state of innocence, this stupidity. If I were used to exercising caution, or had developed the art of not responding to questions—but I barely know anything yet of concealment, of the clandestine.

I discover it there in this nearly empty café, just at the edge of town. The people here are only passing through. They're people on road trips taking a break before resuming their journeys, or gamblers who bet on the horses stopping by just to redeem a winning ticket. Or the glassy-eyed old boozers leaning on the counter, railing against the socialist-communist government. People who don't know us, in any case, for whom we represent nothing and to whom we will say nothing. People who will forget us the moment we leave.

He's already there when I cross the threshold. He

arranged to arrive before me, perhaps to make sure that he wasn't followed, that we weren't seen walking in together.

As I walk toward him, I notice the humid tiles that stick to my shoes, the blue and yellow Formica tables. I imagine the wet sponge that was quickly passed over them as soon as the espresso cups were emptied, the pints of beer consumed. I see old posters of advertisements for Cinzano and Byrrh stuck to the walls, a France from the 1950s. A guy with a stern face stands behind the counter with a ragged towel on his shoulder, as if he just stepped out of a gangster film with Lino Ventura. I feel like an intruder.

Thomas sits at the back of the room trying not to be seen. He's smoking, or rather he nervously pulls on a cigarette (we still smoked in cafés back then). A draft beer sits in front of him (alcohol was also served to minors). As I approach, I see his nervousness, see that it's actually just shyness. I wonder if he feels shame. I want to believe that it's only embarrassment, a question of modesty. I remember, also, that he's reserved in a way that sets him apart. I could be put off, but instead it moves me. Nothing touches me more than cracks in the armor and the person who reveals them.

When I sit across from him, without saying a word, he doesn't lift his head at first, keeping his eyes on the ashtray. He taps on his cigarette to make the ashes fall, but he hasn't smoked it enough. It's a gesture intended to convey composure, but it only makes him appear more vulnerable. He doesn't touch his beer. Me, I stay silent thinking it's up to him to speak first, since he was the one to initiate this strange meeting. I guess that my silence accentuates his discomfort, but what can I do?

I'm trembling. I can feel it in my bones, like when the cold seizes you unexpectedly. I tell myself he has to notice the trembling at least.

Finally, he speaks. I expect something ordinary, to break the ice, something to extricate us from the incongruity of the situation and put us back in the world of the banal. He could ask me how I am, or if I like the place, or if I want something to drink. I would understand those questions and eagerly answer them, happy to let the small talk calm me.

But no.

He says that he has never done this before. He doesn't even know how he dared, how it came to him. He hints at all the questions, all the hesitations, denials, and objections he had to overcome, but adds that he had to do it, that he didn't have a choice. It had become a necessity. The smoke gets in his eyes. He says that he doesn't know how to deal with it, but there it is. It's given to me as a child would throw a toy at the feet of his parents.

He says that he can no longer be *alone with this feeling*.

That it hurts him too much.

With these words he enters into the very heart of the matter. He could have delayed or changed the subject. He could have simply left. He might have wanted to check that he wasn't wrong about me, but he has chosen to offer himself openly to me and to explain, in his own way, what has pushed him toward me at the risk of being compromised, mocked, rejected.

I say: Why me?

It's a way to go straight to the point, to show him the same candor he has shown me. It's also a way to validate everything else, everything that's been said, to get rid of it. To say: I understand, everything is fine, it's fine with me. I feel the same.

However I am still in shock from what he's told me, because nothing could have prepared me for it. It contradicts everything I thought I knew. It's an absolute revelation, a new world. It's also an explosion, a bullet fired next to an eardrum.

But in that split second I somehow instinctively know that I must rise to the occasion, that he would not bear to see me stammering or in a daze, otherwise everything will crumble to the ground.

I figure that a new question might save us from such a disaster.

The question that imposed itself: Why me?

The image doesn't fit: my thick glasses, my stretched-out blue Nordic sweater, the student head slaps, the too-good grades, the feminine gestures. Why me?

He says: Because you are not like all the others, because I don't see anyone but you and you don't even realize it.

24

He adds this phrase, which for me is unforgettable: *Because you will leave and we will stay.*

Even now I remain fascinated by this sentence. Understand, it isn't the premonition that fascinates me, nor even the fact that it has been realized. It's also not the maturity or poignancy implied. It's not the arrangement of the words, even if I'm aware that I probably wouldn't have been able to come up with those exact ones myself. It's the violence that the words carry within them, their admission of inferiority and, at the same time, of love.

He tells me something I did not know: that I will leave.

That my existence will be played out elsewhere, very far from Barbezieux, with its leaden skies and stifling horizon. That I will escape as one does a prison. That I will succeed.

That I will seek out our capital city, that I will make my home there, and find my place.

That I will travel the planet, because I was not made for the sedentary life.

He imagines an ascension, some kind of epiphany. He believes me to have a brilliant destiny, convinced that within our little community nearly forgotten by the gods, there are only a few chosen and that I'm among them.

He thinks that soon I will have nothing to do with this world of my childhood, that it will be like a block of ice detached from a continent.

If he had expressed any of this I would have burst out laughing.

*　　*　　*

As I've said: at that moment in time, I don't have much ambition. I know I can accomplish long and prestigious courses of study, I'm very disciplined, deferential even, but I have no idea where it will lead me. I imagine that I will have to climb the mountain pass, since I have the qualities of a climber, but the peaks remain imprecise and uncertain; in the end my future is in a fog and I don't care about it.

I have no idea that one day I will write books. It's an inconceivable hypothesis. If by some extraordinary chance the idea happened to cross my mind, I would have chased it away. The son of a school principal, an imposter?

Never. Writing books is not a suitable occupation, and above all, it's not a job, because it doesn't earn money. It doesn't offer security or status. It's also not in the real world. Writing is on the outside. Real life you have to touch, you have to grab it. *No, never, my son. Don't even think about it*, I hear my father's voice saying.

And as I said: I had no desire to escape. Later, this desire will invade and overwhelm me. It will begin, in the classic way, with an urge to travel to new places, destinations selected from maps and picture postcards. I will take trains, boats, planes, I will embrace Europe, discover London, a youth hostel next to Paddington Station, a Bronski Beat concert, thrift stores, the speakers of Hyde Park, beer gardens, darts, tawdry nights, Rome, walks among the ruins, finding shelter under the umbrella pines, tossing coins into fountains, watching boys with slicked-back hair whistle at passing girls. Barcelona, drunken wanderings along La Rambla and accidental meetings late on the waterfront. Lisbon and the sadness that's inevitable before such faded splendor. Amsterdam with her mesmerizing volutes and red neon. All the things you do when you're twenty years old. The desire for constant movement will come after, the impossibility of staying in one place, the hatred of the roots that hold you there, *Doesn't matter where you go, just change the scenery*, says the lyric to a song.

I remember Shanghai, the teeming crowd, the ugliness of the buildings, an artificial city that doesn't even preserve the majesty of her river. I remember Johannesburg, its splendor and its poverty. I remember Buenos Aires, people dancing under a volcano, girls with endless legs and older women waiting for the return of their loved ones, the disappeared, a return that will never happen. Later still, the need for exile will put millions of miles and jet lag between France and me, and I will seriously consider moving to Los Angeles for good, never to return. But at seventeen years old, there is none of that.

Thomas Andrieu says that no one can know, everything must stay hidden. That it is the condition: take it or leave it. He puts out his cigarette in the ashtray and finally raises his head. I stare into his eyes, which look somber and determined. I tell him that it's okay, but his requirement, and the burning in his eyes, scare me.

A million questions flash through my mind: How did it begin for him? How and at what age did it reveal itself? How is it that no one can see it on him? Yes, how can it be so undetectable? And then: Is it about suffering? Only suffering? And again: Will I be the first? Or were there others before me? Others who were also secret? And: What does he imagine *exactly*? I don't ask any of these questions, of course. I follow his lead, accepting the rules of the game.

He says: I know a place.

The suddenness of the proposition disconcerts me. We were perfect strangers one hour ago, or at least I thought we were, since I had never noticed his desire for me. I didn't see the looks he had stealthily cast in my direction. I didn't know that he had asked around about me. So, yes, we were perfect strangers, and then just like that, he asks me point-blank to come with him to who knows where, to do who knows what.

I say: I'll follow you.

At that moment, I would have followed him anywhere, done anything he asked.

*   *   *

I'm still not totally convinced it exists, thinking such speed and ease are only for films and bad novels, or in big cities where they're used to cruising and fucking—uncomplicated one-night stands. A couple of years earlier I had watched two strangers meet and leave together. After one look, they disappeared behind a gateway at the edge of the Bordeaux–Saint-Jean train station right near a sex shop. I was fifteen years old and it shocked and troubled me, but mostly I was incredulous. I kept telling myself: You must be mistaken. It's your imagination. Nobody locks themselves into anything like that at first glance.

I'm still there. Still in this innocence. Can you imagine?

He gets up, leaves five francs on the table for the beer he barely touched. I follow him outside. We walk in silence; he's always just a little bit ahead of me. He walks quickly with his shoulders hunched, and it isn't only because of the cold. He lights another cigarette. I envision the knotted muscles of his body, the milky skin dotted with moles. I have to quicken my pace to make up for lagging behind.

To my great surprise, we return to school, but at the last moment, we cut across the gym, which is closed and empty at this hour. At least that's what I suppose. But he has everything planned. He bypasses the wood basketball court, scales a wall, and reaches a small window and pushes it open. He climbs into it. I wonder how he knows about this opening, if perhaps this unlikely route was well planned and already practiced. He gives me a hand so I can climb through the window when it's my turn. I think that's the first contact, his outstretched hand. I never touched him before and then it happens during a break-in.

The place we land is deserted, smelling of teenagers' leftover sweat, pungent and unclean. The floor creaks under our feet. The far corner leads to the locker room. Thomas continues in this direction, up to the cloakroom, past the showers.

Love is made there.

Love, it's mouths that seek, lips that bite, drawing a little blood. His stubble irritates my chin, his hands grab my jaw so that I can't escape.

It's the coarseness of his hair where I slide my fingers, the tautness of his neck. My arms close around him, encircle him to be as close as possible, so that there is no space between us.

It's torsos that join together and then withdraw in a hurry to remove clothing, the Nordic sweater, the T-shirt, so that finally it's skin next to skin. His torso is muscular and hairless, with nipples that are flat and dark. My chest is skinny, not yet deformed as it will be four years later by the blows of an emergency room doctor.

It's skin that is frantically caressed. My fingers find a constellation of moles, just as I guessed, on his back.

It's jeans that we unbutton. I discover his sex, veiny, white, sumptuous. I am enthralled by his sex. It will take many years and many lovers before I ever return to this sense of amazement.

Love, it's taking each other in the mouth, maintaining a certain comportment despite the frenzy. It's exercising restraint not to come, the excitement is so powerful. It's abandonment, that crazy trust in the other.

I guessed that it was not the first time for him. His movements are too sure, too simple not to have been practiced before with someone else, maybe with many others.

And then, he asks me to take him. He says the words, without shame, without ordering me to either. I obey him, though I'm afraid. I know that it can hurt if the other person doesn't know how to do it, that the body can resist.

We make love without a condom.

AIDS is there though. We even know its true identity. It's no longer referred to as the "gay cancer." It's there but we think we are safe from it. We know nothing of the grand decimation that will follow, depriving us of our best friends and old lovers, that will bring us together in cemeteries and cause us to scratch out names in our address books, enraging us with so many absences, such profound loss. It is there but we aren't afraid yet. We believe that we are protected by our youth. We are seventeen years old. You don't die when you are seventeen years old.

Suffering transforms into pleasure.

And then after, fatigue. A gigantic fatigue that leaves us dazed, mute, and dumbfounded. It takes us several minutes to come back to life. We get dressed without looking at each other.

I would like to make a gesture, something resembling tenderness, but I stop myself.

We leave the gym as we came in, sneaking ourselves through the window, and return to the biting cold of winter outside.

He says: Bye.

And then he disappears.

I should be able to stay in this state of ecstasy. Or astonishment. Or let myself be overwhelmed by the incomprehensibility of it all. But the feeling that prevails the moment he disappears is that of being *abandoned*. Perhaps because it is already a familiar feeling.

It was a carnival, one that happened every year during Easter on the Place du Château. There were rides, a carousel with wooden horses, bumper cars; a rifle-shooting game with pink and blue stuffed toys to win; a slide; slot machines; a punching ball to measure your strength; candy stands; the scent of cotton candy and waffles; alcoholic drinks for the grown-ups; a carnie, hidden from sight, who didn't stop barking into a microphone; and the music too loud, all the time. There were no clowns or magicians, no doubt they were too expensive for a town like Barbezieux.

I was seven years old. I pleaded so much that my mother finally gave in and took me. There was very little in the way of amusements near us except for this one carnival once a year.

I was dazzled. I wanted to climb on the carousel over and over, I tried to catch Mickey's tail, I begged to go on every single ride. I was an exhausting child. I didn't notice my mother was worn out. I also didn't notice when she recognized one of our neighbors and stopped to talk with her. I was far too occupied with gnawing on the candied apple she'd bought for me and that I devoured while watching the bumper cars, fascinated by the collisions, and the shouting and electric sparks from above the track. I was so entranced that I let myself get carried away by this crazy messy joyful crowd who paid no attention to a tiny young boy. The crowd pulled me away from my mother. When I finally noticed, it was too late, she was no longer in my sight. Suddenly I realized how exhausted she was. She had just told me, "You tire me out." And in that fraction of a second I decided that she'd abandoned me there because she couldn't take me and my hyperactivity anymore. I became convinced that she'd run off and was never coming back. It was the end. I would be alone forever. I began crying, then screaming, a child's keening lament. I dropped the remains of my candied apple on the ground and went running in the direction I'd seen her last, but she wasn't there. I started running in every direction, colliding into the legs of strangers. Most likely I ran only a few yards but the memory I have is one of an interminable, anarchic, exhausting race. Finally, my mother found me. She grabbed my arm and began to lecture me. She too had been terrified, panicking when she realized that she couldn't find me. She'd searched everywhere, yelling my name, but I hadn't heard her because of the barker with the microphone, the loud music, the laughing crowds. She screamed over the noise that I was absolutely impossible! I couldn't just go away, couldn't just let go of her hand. She yanked even harder, hurting my arm. I could see nothing but her anger, an anger that rendered me speechless. A moment ago I had imagined myself an orphan and when I found my mother again it was only to bear her recriminations.

When Thomas disappears around the corner of the gym, I am seven years old again.

The following days are a nightmare.

I doubt that my lover will come to me, since he's the one who insisted on this wall of silence. The other students would surely not fail to notice if he by chance greeted me, if he happened to say hello, even casually. Because, as I said, we ran in very different circles, a crossing, even an accidental, furtive one, was inconceivable. It was clear to me that it was out of the question to take even the slightest risk.

I understand and yet I can't help but hope for a sign, one only detectable by us, his brushing up against me inadvertently, a glance that no one else can spot, a brief smile. I dream of a brief smile.

But there is nothing. Nothing at all.

Most of the time, he arrives at school at the last moment and leaves as soon as the bell rings. He hardly exits his classroom.

And as for the rare seconds scraped together on the playground, or in the hallway, when we're finally in the same place: total indifference. Worse than coldness. An attentive observer might even discern a certain hostility, a determination to keep his distance.

This coldness mortifies me. It confirms all my worst fears.

I ask myself: Does he regret it? Was it only a stroke of madness for him? A tragic, wrongheaded, even grotesque error? He acts as if nothing happened, or as if everything should be forgotten, buried. It's even worse than being forgotten, it's a denial. And then suddenly, I can't see anything but his rejection. It's as if he's negating everything that transpired between us, one body against the other, as if the image has been completely erased.

To escape this feeling of being excommunicated, I reason with myself: perhaps he was simply disappointed, I didn't live up to what he had imagined. I keep telling myself that despite the evidence, it can be fixed, I can make it up to him. I'm already hoping to be able to beg for another chance. I hang on to the possibility of redemption.

But of course, I come back to my nearsightedness, my lack of muscle tone, the ugly blue Nordic sweater, my off-putting air of superiority; so many defects, so many defeats. I go back to what I was before, the boy who intrigues, not the boy who satisfies. I tell myself that pleasing him was just an illusion, and that pleasure itself lasts only as long as an embrace in a closet.

I discover the pain of waiting, because there is this refusal to admit defeat, to believe that a future where it happens again is possible. I try to convince myself that he'll make some kind of sign in my direction. The memory of our tangled bodies will overcome his resistance, it has to. As he told me himself, it's a question of necessity. You can't fight necessity. If you do, necessity will win.

I discover the pain of missing someone. I miss his skin, his body, which I once possessed and then had taken away from me. It must be given back under threat of madness.

*   *   *

Later I will write about this longing, the intolerable deprivation of the other. I will write about the sadness that eats away at you, making you crazy. It will become the template for my books, in spite of myself. I wonder sometimes if I have ever written of anything else. It's as if I never recovered from it: *the inaccessible other*, occupying all my thoughts.

The death of so many of my friends in my youth will aggravate this tendency. Their premature disappearance will further plunge me into depths of sorrow and uncertainty. I will have to learn how to survive them, and perhaps writing is a good means of survival. A way of not forgetting the ones who have disappeared, of continuing a dialogue.

The source of this missing and longing can be found in this first desertion, this imbecilic burning love.

I discover that absence has a consistency, like the dark water of a river, like oil, some kind of sticky dirty liquid that you can struggle and perhaps drown in. It has a thickness like night, an indefinite space with no landmarks, nothing to bang against, where you search for a light, some small glimmer, something to hang on to and guide you. But absence is, first and foremost, silence. A vast, enveloping silence that weighs you down and puts you in a state where any unforeseeable, unidentifiable sound can make you jump.

In order not to sink completely, I hang on to the memory of his body: his white veiny penis, his moles. This vivid memory saves me from ruin.

It will be nine days before Thomas approaches me again.

Nine days. That number has stayed with me.

We cross paths in a hallway darkened by the winter rain, the kind of rain that invites the night into the day. I am leaving the library again. I checked out a book, I don't remember the title, maybe *Swann's Way* by Proust, which I had tried to read before without success. In any case it is definitely not a contemporary novel, because those are rare. (The National Education board must have thought that they had to lock us in the past, to protect us from the present. They made us learn all the classics and kept us in this state like little scholarly monkeys.) So, as I'm leaving the library, holding the book I've checked out firmly against my side, Thomas walks in my direction, enchanting and petrifying me. I see him put his hand in his back pocket and take something out. It's a piece of paper. He hands it to me quickly, as if hoping not to get caught, and then continues on his way. I guess he waited for a good moment to be alone with me to make his move. I am taken aback by this excess precaution; in another context I would have found it ridiculous. But I understand the fear and panic he carries with him. I know how strong this fear is and also that it can't only be the fear of being caught. It's a fear of himself too. A fear of what he is.

* * *

I wait for the hallways to empty out, making myself late for the class I'm returning to, and I unfold the piece of paper. There is just a place and a time written on it. Nothing else, not my name, no signature. There is no warmth, no good wishes, just the essential information. The piece of paper can never be used as evidence against him. We have a new date.

This time he's chosen a shed next to the soccer field where the sports equipment and uniforms are stored. The field is unoccupied; it's raining so hard that playing any sport right now would be impractical. I run under the downpour, mud clinging to the hem of my pants. When I reach the shed, I notice that the door is ajar. Thomas waits for me inside. His clothes are soaked too; drops of water fall from his hair and roll onto his cheeks. He has just arrived. I ask how he is, how he managed to open the door without the key since these buildings are usually closed to prevent theft. I find out that there is no lock that can resist him. He has been picking locks since he was little, amusing his father and his cousins with his dexterity. They asked him regularly to perform this sleight of hand at the end of Sunday lunches. He's a bit of a magician.

I realize then that we are having our first conversation.

Up until then, he was the only one to speak. At the café,

with the drunks and gamblers, I didn't say a word. Afterward, in the gym, there was only sex. Now here we are talking about how to pick locks, how he discovered he possessed this talent and perfected it. I smile when he tells me the story. It's also the first time I've smiled at him. He smiles back at me. It seems as intimate to me, as magnetic, as skin against skin.

His hair continues to drip water, the wet strands sticking to his forehead. His beauty is devastating. He kneels down on the mattress. I do the same.

I don't say: Why did you wait so long before showing up? Did you hesitate? Did you decide not to see me anymore before changing your mind? I know that I must never ask him these kinds of questions, I can't ever ask him to explain himself, and knowing this crushes me.

I don't say: I missed you. Showing any sentimentality or gushing on my part would horrify him.

I speak of locks. And I have no metaphors. Simply because there are none.

And then silence comes. Our looks shift, shyness and desire masking them. The kisses come. Carnivorous kisses.

As soon as the desire is satisfied, pleasure achieved, our bodies sated, I figure it will be like the last time in the gym: the silence, the faces turned away, the hurried separation. But he has decided otherwise. He says that it would be better to wait since it's still raining too hard and there won't be anyone outside anyway. I understand that he intends to speak.

He says that he lives in Lagarde-sur-le-Né. I know the village; my grandmother died there. I say "village" but there is no real village. It's essentially farmland. There is one country road that leads into town. It was precisely on this road that my grandmother was crushed. It was at the end of the day, at twilight—the hour we call "between a dog and a wolf." She was crossing the street after my grandfather. I may have once known what they were doing there, but I've forgotten. They were most likely meeting up with friends who lived in the area. They parked their car at the side of the road and then had to cross it. He went first, as he always did. She didn't hear the van coming. Though she wasn't hit hard, it was hard enough for her to succumb to her injuries. My grandfather didn't see the collision; his back was turned. He heard the braking and the impact and when he turned back around, her body was on the ground. Her head had hit the pavement. It was this trauma that proved to be fatal. My grandmother was not even sixty years old. I was very young when she died. I don't really have memories of her, I simply recall a blurry image of a gray-haired woman standing behind a bay window, but this is probably a conjured image, it might not even exist. I know the story because it has been recounted to me numerous times, because everyone lamented the negligence. This bad luck, to die on a deserted road that almost no one ever used. It was the fault of the dim light, they said. One minute earlier or later, it never would have happened. I remember this expression, "One minute earlier or later."

Years later, the film director Patrice Chéreau told me (knowing nothing of this drama): People who die from being crushed sometimes do it on purpose. They throw themselves under the wheels of cars. It's particularly true when the accident seems to be incomprehensible, when everyone is convinced that it could have been avoided. He even had a character in his last film, *Persecution*, say something along the same lines: "It suits everyone to believe in an accident. It's less embarrassing than a suicide."

I wonder if my grandmother could have committed suicide. I don't know. I like to believe that she did it, as it would have been the sole act of freedom in her entire existence. A woman who spent her whole life making children (seven in twenty years), raising them, and then being relegated to remain in the shadow of a celebrated and capricious husband.

So Thomas Andrieu lives in this village synonymous in my family with death.

He lives on a farm. His parents are farmers who own a little plot of land. They are modest people who sell the product of their vineyard to cognac distilleries. He corrects himself: Actually the vineyard is just a row of vines surrounded by low walls.

I would like to interrupt to tell him that I understand what he is talking about. In front of my elementary school, on the other side of the main road, there were vines growing on the sloping hillsides. Great tortured gnarled branches that looked like some fabulous beast. At seven or eight years old, I asked to participate in the harvest. As the principal's son, I was told that it wasn't my place but I begged, so they gave in as one does to a child's whim. I was sent to the neighbors who produced the cognac. Look at the well-dressed child "picking the grapes"—lifting up the leaves, untying the clusters, and placing them in a bucket too carefully. As always, this child isn't aware that he's being favored, that his presence is only tolerated, since it is actually real and hard work. Work that requires concentration, agility, and endurance. The Spaniards next to me have been brought in for two or three weeks to collect the grapes, a cheap and docile workforce coming from Bilbao or Sevilla. I like the happy Spaniards with their weather-beaten skin. I understand nothing they say. In the evenings they meet up at a campsite of caravans they have parked in the fields. No doubt they are being exploited but they don't complain. With the fruits of their labor, a famous brandy is manufactured. A very expensive liqueur exported around the entire world, consumed in China and Japan, generating profits they will never see.

As the day ends, I am the amusing child in the tub with his bare feet and legs, stamping on the grapes to crush the skins. It's the end of the season, and everyone gathers around a long table. People are speaking loudly, drinking, laughing, playing the guitar, for the last time before the Spaniards leave to return the following autumn, or possibly never. For me the separation is heartbreaking. Later I sit in the distillery in front of the stills and copper pipes, waiting for the smoke to escape. It's called "the angel's share." I am the child who is waiting for the share of the angels. My father was amused to have his son participate in this ritual, but he had already repeated many times over that he didn't want this life for me. No land or field work, no manual labor. It was out of the question for him that I should be a member of the working class.

So I stay silent when Thomas talks about the vineyard.

He says that he raises cows too, that they have quite a few. This time I speak up to tell him that I know how to milk cows. There was a stable in the village I grew up in. Every other night, we would go to buy fresh milk (warm, since it had just come out of the animal). I was fascinated by the sight of the farmer kneading the udder to extract the milk. I immediately asked her to show me how to do it. She taught me the gestures, and I was good at it. It was like a game for me, and I'm good at games. And I wasn't afraid of the cows, not afraid when they tapped me with their hooves and swished their tails. They had to understand that I wasn't afraid so that they would let themselves go. When I tell the story now of how I happened to possess this skill, no one believes me, convinced that I'm just inventing one of my stories. A drawback of my habit of embellishing.

The moment I tell Thomas, he cracks up laughing. He can't imagine me sitting on a little stool, my fingers kneading the teats of a cow. It makes me angry. He says that I'm not that boy there, that it's impossible. He says I'm a boy of books, from somewhere else.

This is important: he sees me in a certain way, a way he will never deviate from. In the end, love was only possible because he saw me not as who I was, but as the person I would become.

The rain continues to pound against the roof of the shed. We are alone in the world. I've never enjoyed the rain so much.

He says that he loves the farm, the land. But he aspires to something else. I reply that he *will do* something else since he has embarked on the studies that will allow him to, that once he has his bac in his pocket, he can try medicine, or the pharmacy, or whatever he wants. He responds that he isn't sure it's possible because he's the only boy in the family. He has two sisters and the farm will die if he doesn't take it over. The idea offends me. I tell him we're not still living in the fifties. That sons don't necessarily have to take over from their fathers, that farming is no longer hereditary and agriculture is doomed to die anyway, it's a dead end. I tell him he has to think about his future. His expression darkens. He says he doesn't like when I talk like that.

The rain lets up a little. He gets up to go look outside across the fields, at the muddy, almost gray, lawn, the uncertain boundaries, the rusty poles and loose nets tossed about by the gusts of wind, the deserted bleachers; all this desolation. He puts on his jeans. He's still shirtless, in spite of the cold. I get up too. I start to press myself against his back, wrapping my arms around his pelvis. He tenses at the contact, repelling my tenderness. I say: It's so you'll be less cold.

He gently disengages from my embrace, grabs his T-shirt and sweater, and puts them back on.

Obviously he's still bothered by what I said about leaving the farm, "killing the father." He seems to think that I know nothing about it. He also thinks that I don't realize the violence of such an act. He's offended by what he views as carelessness on my part.

He says that for me things are simple, that everything will be fine, that I will get out of it, it's already written, that there's

46

nothing to worry about, the world will greet me with open arms. Whereas for him there's a barrier, an impenetrable wall, forbidding him to deviate from what has been predetermined.

Whenever he mentions this question of the forbidden I will try in vain to show him that he's wrong.

The rain stops and suddenly we feel less protected, less cut off from others. It seems to us that someone could show up. I notice the agitation of his features, his leg twitching. He must get out of this place, leave right now. It's become an imperative. Before he opens the door I dare to ask: Will we see each other again soon?

He doesn't hesitate.

He says: Yes, obviously.

I hear the "obviously," which signals that a story has begun, that we will not return to the way it was before, that everything will not stop. I could cry but I know it's too sentimental.

I say: If you want, the next time we can meet at my place.

He's unable to mask his surprise, or his reluctance. I form several theories—he prefers unlikely, complicated places, a room is too expected, predictable, bourgeois; he prefers neutral territory, a place where we are equal, to play at the home field of your opponent puts you at a disadvantage; he's not sure if he wants to become acquainted with this intimate place, it will turn a corner in the course of our involvement.

I figure that the only real acceptable objection to his reluctance must be material, concrete, almost trivial. I say: My parents work, they're almost never there, we won't be bothered. I'm counting on his fear of being found out. He says okay, that he will come.

A day and time are set.

He tells me to leave the shed first. He'll wait a few minutes, to lock the door. He stands back a little at a distance as if to avoid any possible outpouring of emotion, any tenderness. For the duration of our relationship, Thomas will be wary of anything tender.

And come to think of it, he won't ever invite me to his place, not even once. I will never see the grazing animals, the farmhouse or the vineyards surrounding it. I will never see its interior, the cool tiles, the plaster walls, the dark rooms with low ceilings, the heavy, solid furniture. (I've invented all this, you know, precisely because I never saw it.) I won't ever meet his parents, not even from afar. There will be no handshake, no pleasantries exchanged between us; I presume that he would never have spoken to them about me, even inadvertently (he's not the inadvertent type). I would have liked to have seen which one he most resembled. Obviously, I wouldn't have betrayed him. I would've played the role of the nice schoolmate. I'm capable of playing any part.

One day I decided to go to his village, Lagarde, on my

own. It was a day when I knew he wouldn't be there so I roamed around trying to figure out which house and family were his. I was tempted to ask an old man sitting on a bench in front of the church, but then I changed my mind, feeling suddenly embarrassed by my recklessness, and left.

On the day itself, moments before Thomas rings the bell to my house, I have an anxiety attack. I shaved twice, even though I have almost no beard to speak of, and cut myself, leaving a gash along the bottom of my left cheek. I put the styptic pencil on it, but it didn't help. I'm convinced that I'm now horribly disfigured. I put cologne on too, which I normally don't do, and it makes me reek. It's my father's cologne, a heady earthy scent dominated by musk. I put on dark clothes—black jeans, a navy sweater—that I think Thomas will like, and then at the last minute change back into my original outfit of blue jeans and a green shirt. I counted the hours and minutes before he showed up, watched from behind the curtains by the window so he wouldn't see me. I really regretted not knowing how to smoke. I thought a cigarette would serve me well at that moment, since people say it helps calm the nerves.

He doesn't notice my excitement when he comes in, or any of the efforts I've made either. It's only the house that interests him; he walks around it as though it's a minefield. He mentions nothing of the size or the light or the décor, he says simply that there are a lot of books, that he has never seen so many books. Not wanting to linger he asks to see my room. We have to go up two flights of stairs.

The room is quite big, cut in half by a partition that separates the bedroom from the desk area. It's in the attic so the windows are small. There is old cream-colored carpeting on the floor scattered with stains left by muddy boots. Posters of the pop singer Jean-Jacques Goldman are taped up on the wall. Thomas lowers his eyebrows and gives me a look, intending to poke fun at me. He claims that Goldman is music for girls. Annoyed, I tell him he's wrong, that he has to listen closely to the lyrics. He says the lyrics aren't important, only the music counts and the energy that you get from it. He listens to the rock band Téléphone. I don't argue with him about Téléphone's lyrics because he would think I was trying to teach him a lesson. For him in that instant I am hopelessly girly.

If I had known it then, I could have told him that Marguerite Duras was crazy for the Hervé Vilard ballad "Capri, It's Over." In *Yann Andrea Steiner*, she wrote:

Yes. One day it will happen, one day you'll miss horribly what you described as "unbearable"—what we tried to do, you and I, in the summer of 1980, that summer of wind and rain.

50

Sometimes it happens by the sea. When the beach grows empty, at nightfall. After the children's summer camps have gone. All over the sands a shriek goes up, saying that Capri is over. It was the city of our early love, *but now it's over.* Over.

It's suddenly awful. Awful. Whenever it happens it makes you want to weep, run away, die, because Capri has revolved with the earth, revolved toward the forgetting of love.

I also could have spoken to him about what the director François Truffaut had to say through the character Mathilde, played by Fanny Ardant, in *The Woman Next Door*, since I had just seen the film.

I only listen to songs because they tell the truth. The more stupid they are, the more honest. And incidentally, they are not stupid. What do they say? They say: "Don't leave me . . . Your absence has broken my life . . . ," or "I'm an empty house without you . . . Let me become a shadow of your shadow . . . ," or "Without love, you are nothing at all . . ."

To which the character Bernard, played by Gérard Depardieu, responds:

Okay, Mathilde, I have to go now.

When he comments on my musical tastes, I sense in Thomas the same weary disdain, the same desire to move on to something else. He goes back to the books—this crazy number of books in the house neatly lined up or stacked in piles. All of a sudden I see a sort of admiration return to his face, but it's a painful admiration; what he likes about me is also what keeps me separate from him.

He says that he wants to suck me off, that it can't wait. One would swear that this need just came to him, out of nowhere, that seconds before it didn't exist, that it hasn't been building up for days. He throws me on the bed, unfastens my jeans, and lowers my briefs. If he could, he would have torn them, it's like a scene from a straight porno film, the girl who gets her white cotton panties ripped off. I let myself grow in his mouth. At first I don't dare look at him, telling myself he wouldn't want to be watched while doing such a thing. I'm still thinking that everything has to be done according to him and his desires, his inhibitions too. Finally, slowly, I raise my head and lean back on my elbows and take in the sight of him. I'm struck by his voracity. He's like a ravenous child who has just been given food and prefers to choke on it. I'm not sure where this need for another man's sex comes from but I sense that on the other side of all the repression and self-censoring there exists an equally powerful fervor.

*   *   *

During the next several weeks, I begin to wonder if he chose me only because I was available, because I was the ideal vehicle through which to fulfill his repressed desires, because he hadn't yet found others like me. I will repeat to myself: I am for him a boy he fucks, nothing more. I'm reduced to a body, a penis, a function.

Before I forget: Regarding uncomplicated sex, many years later I will spend time with porn actors. I'll even live with one for many months in California, the mecca of the porn industry. I will go regularly to film shoots and watch the actors warm up, fake attraction, grab each other, get a rhythm going, freeze for photographs, and then resume with the panting as if nothing happened. I'll become close to these guys who have sex for a few hundred dollars. I'll discover that certain ones do it just to make a living, and for them it's a job like any other—they're just managing with what nature has given them. Others are like machines. They spend hours each day at the gym for the sole purpose of having the perfect body, or, more precisely, a body that corresponds to the standards of the business. They shoot themselves up with steroids, their shoulders riddled with scars they go to the tanning salon; it's a constant competition on set. And then, finally, there are the ones who derive pleasure from having multiple partners and frolicking in front of the camera. Sometimes they even fall under the spell of their partner of the day, bringing more truth to the performance perhaps. They are all crazy about their bodies. They all claim that for them, sex is a vital need, like a drug. Their vulnerability touches me.

Thomas undresses, leaving his clothes around the room. He wants to be naked himself so that our skin touches (he has no problem with nudity and teaches me to be less afraid of mine). He caresses me with hands that know exactly what to do. He bites my hips, my torso. He groans, no longer able to contain it, a sound that he releases maybe without even realizing it himself; he moves me tremendously. As I've said, nothing in life moves me more than these moments of pure abandon, of self-oblivion.

He lies on his stomach, arching slightly for me. I see the hair that runs down the edge of his backside. I slide my tongue there and he groans again, trembling. I see the gooseflesh on the surface of his skin. In front of my eyes is one of the Goldman posters, all around me are the artifacts of a teenage boy's room. A boyhood I'm in the process of annihilating.

After, he starts talking again. It's like a gate has opened. It seems that Thomas doesn't speak a lot. The meals in his family are passed in silence. The evenings are short, since they are often exhausted and have to go to bed early. At school, I've noticed that he always holds back a little, dragging on a cigarette and letting others do the talking. Sometimes he doesn't even bother to act as though he were listening. I remember loving this about him, his air of isolation. Now he feels he should speak to me, but perhaps it is only for himself, like throwing a bottle into the sea, or keeping a diary or whispering into the ground like King Midas's barber because it's just too much to keep to himself.

He tells me about his little sisters, Nathalie and Sandrine. Sixteen and eleven years old respectively.

Nathalie is a year and a half younger than he is. It made sense for a second child to be born so soon after the first one, but he says she doesn't look anything like him. She takes after their father. She has his light eyes, his strength.

I say: So you, do you take after your mother then? He says yes, he has her dark complexion. He adds: Something of the foreigner. I don't understand the phrase. I don't ask for an explanation, believing that explanations will come later.

Nathalie quit her general studies to go to a secretarial school where she also boards. She returns on Friday nights and helps with the farmwork on the weekends. There is always something to do.

He says that they don't get along very well, that they

don't have good chemistry; he finds her too practical, too planted in real life, always lecturing everyone as though she were already old.

Sandrine, he adores, the baby of the family who arrived late, unplanned. His face lights up when he speaks of her, though it seems that her coming into the world left his parents stunned. The doctors had given them the news immediately: the baby was born with Down syndrome. There weren't ultrasounds at the time, so nothing had been detected. Sandrine is permanently stuck in a childlike state. Their father doesn't know what to do with her, and Nathalie isn't always nice. She becomes easily exasperated by the little one's slowness. As for the mother, she doesn't say anything but has carried with her a palpable sadness since her younger daughter was born.

Thomas is the eldest and the only boy, which he suggests gives him a certain responsibility.

I'm the youngest of my family. My brother is pursuing advanced studies and will soon write his thesis and become a doctor of mathematics, publishing articles in international journals that are inaccessible to laymen and attending conferences around the world. Imagine what it was like growing up after him. As good a student as I was, unfavorable comparisons were made regularly. It's why, I explain to Thomas, the destiny he envisions for me can be considered only second-rate compared to the one that awaits my older brother. He assures me that I'm wrong.

I add that I almost had a little brother. My mother became pregnant seven years after I was born, but the pregnancy didn't go to term. The miscarriage happened very late, almost in the sixth month, and the ordeal left my mother drained and given to despair, though she never said a word on the subject. (No, not even one—such remarkable discipline.) He would have been named Jérôme or Nicolas. Often I think of this little brother I never had. Thomas says: You see how we come from different worlds. *Worlds that have nothing to do with each other.*

I come back to his mother; she is the one who most interests me. Right away he tells me that she is Spanish. She came to France twenty years ago with her brothers, who had found work on a farm. They weren't exiled because of the Franco regime, or a desire to escape single-party rule—the censorship, the crooked courts, the despotism—no, it was just a young girl and her brothers who knew nothing but work and heard that there was some to be found on the other side of the border. She immediately met twenty-five-year-old Paul Andrieu. The brothers ended up going back, but she stayed.

I ask him: Where in Spain? He brushes my question away with a sweep of his hand, assuring me that I wouldn't know it. I insist, so he gives me the name: Vilalba. I say: Yes, it's in Galicia, in the Lugo province. He's surprised: But how do you know it? I say: It's on the way to Santiago de Compostela. He asks if I've ever been there. I tell him no, never, but I read about it in a book and remembered it. He makes fun of me, saying: I was *sure* you were a boy like that, one who knows things just because you read it in a book. He then becomes despondent and adds: But what's worse is that if someone asked both of us, I'm pretty sure you would be able to talk about it way better than I could.

Once I become a novelist, I'll write about places I've never been, places I only read on a map and liked the sound of. For example, my novel *A Moment of Abandon* takes place in Falmouth, on the coast of Cornwall, England, where I've never stepped foot. Nevertheless, people who read it are convinced I know it like the back of my hand. Some have even gone so far as to say that the town is *exactly* as I have described it, that such accuracy is striking. I explain that in general it's the *likelihood* that actually matters more than the truth, that the feeling counts more than accuracy, and above all that a place is not a question of topography but rather the way that we describe it—not a photograph but an impression. When Thomas tells me that his mother comes from Vilalba, I immediately visualize a young girl with medium-long hair and black eyes, dressed in a white linen dress, alone on a paved lane, crushed by the heat—and then a church on Sunday morning with the faithful attending mass; also a castle-like fortress where children go to play hide-and-seek, the girl joining them; and hotels on the outskirts of the city for the devout traveler passing through. A fossilized world. I'm convinced that this image is true. And even if it isn't, the hope is that the reader *sees* the girl and in so doing will *see* the town.

He went there many times in the summer during his childhood and adolescence. The visits were always very short because it was impossible to leave the farm for too long. The young apprentice appointed to take care of the farm on such occasions couldn't do everything, the animals required too much attention, the crops could potentially be lost. The family would take the car, first the green Simca 1100, and later the Peugeot 305 Break (how do I remember that?), the three kids in back and the suitcases strapped to the roof. The heat was unbearable so his father would put tea towels on the windows to block out the sun. Every couple of hours they'd pull over at a rest stop to eat sandwiches that had been wrapped in aluminum foil that morning, or to stretch their legs, go to the bathroom, or fill up the tank. Then they'd get right back on the road. The radio was left on, though most of the time there'd be no signal. The songs came in choppy and inaudible, the endings of all the jokes cut off, and they never listened to the news. It seemed like an interminable journey.

*   *   *

His mother's family still lives in Vilalba. The brothers married and have kids. All the kids have cousins who live within a mile. The reunions are always joyous and the good-byes bittersweet, everyone regretting they have so little time together. Thomas says that he doesn't know Vilalba very well because they usually just stay at the house for endless conversations, punctuated by laughter and complaints, long lunches and drawn-out dinners. He says that for him Spain is just people in his family who love one another, who eat and drink and cut each other off in conversation until night falls.

I say: Is that the reason you said *something of the foreigner*?

He says: Yes, dark eyes, olive skin. And the feeling of never quite belonging, of being a person uprooted, as if, maybe, who knows, a sense of not belonging is something one inherits.

I don't ask him if he also has his mother's fragility, even though I've been dying to ask ever since he told me that his sister has their father's strength. He would refuse to answer the question anyway because it's too intimate. It would require a confession on his part, or at least introspection. But I'm convinced that the fineness of his frame comes from her, and his nonchalance too.

*   *   *

He says: What I didn't inherit from her is faith. His mother is very religious, a practicing Catholic who goes to church every Sunday and sometimes even more often, especially since his little sister was born, to demand an explanation from God. Why did he send her this test? Or: How can she find the courage to go on, to be a good mother, in spite of everything? She wears a medallion of the Blessed Virgin around her neck and, of course, always carries a rosary that she rolls around between her fingers; a cross is affixed to the wall above the bed in the master bedroom. She even went so far as to tack a poster of Jesus in the manger to the dining room wall, next to the sideboard. He says that he's grown up with all that. I say: Religious knickknacks, you mean? He tells me not to use that word. He's not a believer himself, but he respects his mother's faith and admits that he pretends to believe so as not to hurt her. It's like that. His mother needs to convince herself that her son is on the right path.

For a long time I wondered if this oppressive religious ideology—the deliverance from evil as a divine principle drummed in day after day, the biblical message of fixed gender roles that his mother internalized, the sanctification of stable relationships as practiced by this unblemished family—could have exercised an influence on a child forbidden to rebel. I think, probably, yes.

He clarifies that he followed the catechism and took holy communion, as was the tradition.

I surprise him by telling him that it is one thing we have in common.

When I was six years old, all my friends began going for religious instruction on Wednesday afternoons, telling my brother and me how much fun they had there. We were forbidden to even enter a church, let alone follow the teachings of a priest! It was quite the transgression for me the day that, unbeknownst to my father, I showed up for class with the group. The priest was surprised to see me, almost suspecting some kind of scam. I assured him that I had my parents' permission. (Already I was able to lie with impressive self-assurance.) At the end of the meeting, the priest accompanied me back to school. My father raised hell when I returned. He had been looking for me everywhere, beside himself with worry. When he saw me holding the hand of this man of God, it wasn't relief that he felt (or if it was, it was very brief); in his eyes I could clearly identify a look of pure wrath. The priest, however, had a modest triumph when I spoke up and said that I loved being in the church and that I wished to continue the instruction. For four years, I would attend class every Wednesday and go to mass on Sunday morning, but the enthusiasm I'd felt in the beginning quickly gave way to tedium. The magnanimity my father had shown was in fact a form of perversity. He made me go all the way, insisting I never miss a meeting. By the time I was ten years old and took my first communion, I detested God, the priests, and the church. Well played, Papa.

I tell Thomas in a joking voice: You see? We aren't so different.

This memory brings me back to the idea of fathers. I realize that Thomas speaks little of his, though he certainly evokes his type, his robustness, and the difficulty he had accepting his daughter's disability. I imagine a handsome man, taciturn and frugal. I suppose that he's a man essentially consumed by work, determined to keep the farm going. But I know nothing of the rapport between him and his son. Thomas says: It's hard to know what he's thinking. It's an elegant way of suggesting that his father isn't affectionate, tender, or reassuring, that he remains aloof, that what he offers is a mix of reserve and unspoken pride for his son. I know what that's like, to be the son of a man like that. I wonder if it's cold fathers who make the sensitive sons.

Thomas and I lie on the bed, my head resting on his chest. I wonder how we came to be in this position. I assume that it happened through the conversation. Not far from us stands a mirror that I usually use to look at myself in the morning, to see how I'm dressed and to comb my hair. I use it now to contemplate our reflection. In this position I suddenly understand that I've changed—aged somehow. I'm no longer a neurotic, frightened, easily insulted boy, but rather a boy who's thinking, who's been awakened. It's something that comes from using the body. From stirring up desire, sharing oneself with another, finding victory over a kind of solitude. Of course I can't say anything *on the outside*, it's part of the contract, but I believe that the change in me is visible, that if one looks closely, one can see a difference. It's bursting out of me.

Recently when I was going through some papers from the desk in my childhood room after my mother decided to "redo the place and get rid of useless things," I came across two photos. The first was dated freshman year, the second was from the summer when I took the bac. In the first image, the young man appears stunted, with slumped shoulders and an anxious look in the eyes. In the second one, he's completely different, a smiling youth with sun-kissed skin. Of course circumstances played a role, but I'm convinced that it was this hidden love that accounted for the transformation.

Thomas looks at the watch on his wrist. He wears a Casio digital. I noticed it at our first meeting, thinking I would like one too. He immediately gets up, forcing me to give up the cushion of his chest. He says that he has to go, his father is waiting for him, that he's already late, something to do with the vines. He puts his clothes back on in a hurry. I protest, telling him that the bus won't come for another half hour, that he can stay a little bit longer, but he tells me that he didn't take the bus. He has a Suzuki 125 that he parked up the street. I don't remember ever seeing him with a helmet. He says that he rides without it most of the time, that he never runs into cops on the country roads. I say: Will you take me for a ride one of these days? I expect the raised shoulders and the smirk, reminding me of the rules. Instead he says: You want to? I believe that yes, definitely, something is changing.

He will keep his promise. A few weeks later he'll take me for a ride. He'll pick me up at the edge of town, with a helmet this time. I don't know if it's as a precaution, to respect the law, or so that we won't be recognized, but I get on the back of the bike and hold on to him. We drive at high speed along back roads, through woods, vineyards, and oat fields. The bike smells like gasoline and makes a lot of noise, and sometimes I'm frightened when the wheels slip on the gravel on the dirt road, but the only thing that matters is that I'm holding on to him, that I'm holding on to him *outside*.

In the meantime, he takes off, walks down the stairs, barely saying goodbye before leaving. When the door closes, the silence is heavy enough to make your knees buckle. The trace of his scent, an intimate mixture of cigarettes and sweat, is the only thing that saves me.

And after? There are more secret meetings, mostly in my room for practical reasons. The more last-minute ones require inventiveness, organization, and caution; sometimes we have the impression that we are coconspirators. Back then there were no cell phones, so I had to call him at his house. When I would hear a voice I didn't know, I often hung up, but sometimes I introduced myself as someone else; after all, Thomas was allowed to have a friend named Vincent! Or then again, I would leave a note in his locker at school with a day and a time, but no signature or any other identifying sign; he responded using the same methods. Sometimes it happened that we set a date for the next time as we were leaving the room, but that was rare, as if there were something vulgar about it, that it would reduce our relationship to a mere erotic obsession.

We skip classes too, pretending to be sick. He says this will raise suspicion and on these days, he is always nervous.

We make love.

I slip down the straps of his tank top. It seems to me that there is no other gesture more sensual, more stirring.

He runs the flat of his hand across my back, caressing my stomach, my hips.

He hands me his cigarette so that I can take a drag. I immediately start coughing. Pathetic. I give a little lick to every one of the moles on his body. I count thirty-two of them. I change his bandage. He was injured by a vine branch that has given him a deep cut on his thigh.

I watch him doze and then his face rolls over to the left, instantly waking him up. He puts the headphones from his Walkman on my ears. He wants me to listen to Bruce Springsteen.

A little tipsy from the half bottle of wine we snuck upstairs, he dances in front of me, listening to the muffled echo of the song. I feel like I'm dreaming.

The rest of the time we stay in bed, kissing, sucking, and fucking.

One day I suggest we go to the movies. I've prepared my argument well: There's hardly ever anyone at the Club, the town theater, especially at the afternoon showings, and the rare spectator is older anyway, we won't risk being recognized. I propose that he go in first, during the previews, and if he doesn't come out after five minutes, I'll know that it's safe to go in. He can see I've thought of everything. I reply that with him I have to. He asks if I'm reproaching him. I say: No, I just haven't forgotten everything you told me that first day in the café with the gamblers and drunks.

I discovered the cinema four years earlier when we first moved to Barbezieux from the village where we lived above the school with the linden trees. It was a small theater, with only a few seats, but to a child from the village, a boy who had to go to bed at eight thirty every night regardless of his pleas and ploys, a boy who had never in his life seen a film before, it was a new world.

From the beginning, I loved the darkened rooms, the deep, soft brown velvet seats that rocked back (brown was not considered a terrible color back then), the giant screen (giant in my memory at least; in reality, probably a little less so), the smell of popcorn (and of mustiness, since a constant humidity prevailed). I even loved the classic animated Jean Mineur ad where a smiling kid rides into a theater on an undulating film strip and then throws his ice pick into a target to hit the number 1,000, causing a phone number to appear, signaling the start of the movie.

At twelve or thirteen years old, I didn't go to see the films intended for my age, the animated films of Walt Disney for example. I didn't like action films, or science fiction, or even the French teen romantic comedy *La Boum,* which every teenager knew by heart. They didn't interest me. No, I chose the films for *old people.* Films by François Truffaut, André Téchiné, Claude Sautet, scandalous films too, like *The Wounded Man* by Patrice Chéreau and *Possession* by Zulawski. When I admit this to Thomas he says: That doesn't surprise me.

Even so he adds: You really went to see *The Wounded Man?* I respond that it was one of the biggest shocks I have ever felt. For the first time, I saw homosexuality represented on-screen in a raw, direct, and uninhibited way. I tell Thomas about the filth and urgency of the train station, the promiscuity of the urinals, the medley of whores and pushers, the very distinct sense one has that everything stinks of shit and semen. I tell him about the trafficking of feelings, the life at the margins, the bodies that seek, press against each other violently, and then separate. I feel his disgust. He says that it's not *that*. . . . He doesn't say: It's not *the homosexuality*. He can't even say the word; in fact, he will never once say it. He says: It's a disgusting portrayal. I remember this expression "disgusting portrayal" that he used, instead of "unhappy portrayal." There are some who have criticized Chéreau in the same way. I tell Thomas that he's mistaken, that it's a love story above all, about the passion that one young man can have for another. I talk about the purity of that kind of crazy love. He tells me that he will never see the film.

*   *   *

I don't know at the time that the writer Hervé Guibert will become an important writer for me. Six months later, I will discover *The Remarkable Adventures* and the passage about the desire to merge with his lover will annihilate me.

I will discover that these books speak to me, and speak *for* me (and will become aware of the power of literary minimalism, the neutral voice that's closer to reality). Six months later, Guibert will announce he's dying of AIDS. I'll wonder then if *The Wounded Man* was a premonition or if, on the contrary, it showed the last glimmer of free love— a love shown without constraint or morality or fear—before the great massacre.

I also don't know then that I will meet Patrice Chéreau one day and work with him. He will adapt one of my novels, a story about brothers and illness and the body as it approaches death. It will be like a circle closing twenty years later.

As this winter of 1984 is coming to an end, the film I'm dying to see is Coppola's *Rumble Fish*, a sequel of sorts to *The Outsiders*, which came out a few months before. I loved that tale of idle youth, the strength of the bonds forged in adolescence, its freedom, starring all the young male actors who will go on to define eighties Hollywood: Tom Cruise, Patrick Swayze, Matt Dillon, Rob Lowe. I loved these bad boys with their slicked-back hair, who were really the little brothers of the boys in *Rebel Without a Cause*. Most of all, I loved C. Thomas Howell, who played Ponyboy. I remember with confounding precision the physical sensation of the "love at first sight" that hit me. It would take me weeks to get rid of this feeling and acknowledge how perfectly absurd it was. Incidentally, I realized *after the fact* that Thomas looked like him (I wondered if it was my unconscious talking but immediately dismissed the thought). When I tell him that *Rumble Fish* was filmed in black and white, he says: We can't see something like that. We aren't our parents.

Instead, we buy tickets for Brian De Palma's *Scarface*, even though it got terrible reviews. It's gratuitously violent, with unnecessarily coarse language and a flashy aesthetic. But of course it's Thomas who's right. The film is a masterpiece, a vicious fable about the corruption of money. While the credits roll he says: That scene with the chain saw was great, wasn't it? I look at him and joke: Yeah, I almost grabbed you at that moment. He smiles back at me and I receive his smile like a gift. There weren't many times Thomas smiled at me like that. It wasn't his way.

He remembers a line. I say: Which one? He says: I have hands made for gold and they're in shit.

*   *   *

Some time later, he and I will find ourselves again in the same place, surrounded by other people, but this time it'll be unintentional, and that will make all the difference.

I was invited to a birthday party. I hesitated before going. I didn't care for celebrations or parties (I've barely changed in that regard). The previous weekend I had caused a scandal because of my dislike for supposedly festive gatherings.

It was a wedding, and one of my cousins was the groom. First, everyone had to go to the church and listen to the bon mots of a sweaty priest, pose for pictures during the walk, scribble best wishes for the family's eternal joy on glossy paper, and then head to a poorly heated multipurpose room to drink cheap wine from white plastic cups and consume peanuts purchased in bulk. Everything reeked of savings—not poverty so much as mediocrity, which struck me as less forgivable. Later the pack moved to a dubious bar in the middle of nowhere, in a county where my father had once taught. I remember the greasy laughter, the screaming conversations, the sweaty brows and stained shirts of my uncles—all this bawdy, overcrowded frivolity. There were the games that still make me feel ashamed even now when I think about them. With her eyes blindfolded, the wife tried to recognize her own husband by feeling the calves of five random men, or another game where she pushed an apple across the floor with a banana dangling down between her legs by a string tied around her waist. The absolute vulgarity of it horrified me. Sitting next to me at the table was one of my cousins, barely fourteen years old, who was recounting his (presumably imaginary) sexual exploits to one of his prepubescent friends. He kept prodding me to share the exact details of my own sexual conquests. (I was tempted to say, I suck cocks, what else do you want to know?) Later the wedding singers, dressed like mechanics out on the town or salesmen who've been a little heavy-handed with the brilliantine, bellowed out old love songs, butchering the classics beyond recognition. At the stroke of eleven, the forty-year-olds started to shimmy to the sound of "The Duck Dance" while the ageless widows contemplated them with smug smiles. I had only one desire: to escape. And that's exactly what I did. I went to find my father and asked him to take me back to the house. My tone must have made an impression because, probably not wanting to create a scene, he did what I asked without argument. On the way home, I swore to myself that I would never be in the same situation again.

A teenage birthday party is far from a wedding, but you can easily slip into triviality or boredom; age doesn't matter much in that regard. I know that what I've written has probably given the impression that I was a haughty young boy, a bit too delicate for the world (and no doubt I was, at least in part). But looking back on it, I think it was simply a fear of crowds, their movements, the inherent potential to transform into a mob, that pushed me toward this misanthropy.

This particular night was basically a gathering of high school students. I recognized a few faces. A pretty, popular girl who was friends with Nadine was celebrating her eighteenth birthday (the moment when one becomes *of age*, that critical milestone that says you are now officially grown, as if before this you were insignificant—a noncitizen. I've always been amused by these artificial frontiers). It was actually Nadine who'd insisted that I come with her, telling me that I wasn't social enough, that real life was not lived in books, that there was nothing wrong with a little lightness, a little carefree partying. She was right. Maybe if I'd listened to her a lot earlier, I wouldn't have missed out on my youth.

Here's the scene: A newly constructed house on the road that leads to Cognac. A large dining room with the furniture taken out, beige tiles, crepe paper hanging from the patio doors and light fixtures, a strobe light. But apart from all that, the atmosphere is fairly subdued. The outdoor lighting in the back garden makes the lawn look even more green. There are more than thirty boys and girls, a few with bleached blond hair and cropped jeans and ankle socks; some are in sweatshirts, others in jackets with epaulets and jodhpurs. Swaths of fluorescent color mix with goth looks. While the soundtrack plays, everyone dances to "Wake Me Up Before You Go-Go" by Wham or "Footloose" by Kenny Loggins. We all sing along to "The Very First Time" by Jeanne Mas and slow-dance to "Time After Time" by Cyndi Lauper. Someone throws in a little unexpected but welcome melancholy with Nena's "99 Luftballons."

It's during the dying notes of this song that Thomas appears. I didn't see him come in, but all of a sudden he's there in the middle of the room. From then on he occupies all the space, claiming it for himself. You would swear that the light went out on everyone else, or at least dimmed. (It reminds me of a screen test I saw once that James Dean did for *Rebel Without a Cause*. All the kids are gathered in a room; they're healthy and attractive, their faces lined up like they're in an El Greco painting, and then Jimmy walks in. Through the lens of the camera he looks smaller than the others, a little stoop shouldered and bookish, with a slight smirk on his face, and you can't take your eyes off him. He makes everyone else disappear. I've probably embellished the scene in retrospect, though I do believe that there are certain men who eclipse everyone else in the room and leave you breathless.)

*   *   *

I didn't expect Thomas to be there, and my first reaction to seeing him is surprise. I didn't even know that he was invited (but why on earth would I have been warned? Who would have warned me?). When I saw him the day before, he didn't say anything about this birthday party (but then again he doesn't owe me anything; our relationship was founded on this absence of obligation). I didn't mention anything to him either. Obviously if we knew, one of us wouldn't have come. The truth is, I never expected to see him at this kind of thing. He is so unsociable and aloof at parties, so out of place in that kind of setting. There's something off, uncomfortably incongruous, about seeing him here.

He hasn't spotted me yet, still not having quite joined the party. He casually lights a cigarette, looks around, and is quickly joined by a couple of friends from his class I noticed earlier. They shake hands in a lazy way, the way you do with close friends with whom you have nothing to prove. Immediately it makes me think of the world I'm excluded from, the friendships he's developed, all the ordinary days that have nothing to do with me. The friends, the handshakes, crystallize it. I'm from a world that is underground, unique and invisible. Ordinarily this would make me feel happy, but tonight it makes me feel like a fool.

*   *   *

All the same, there is often a staggering intimacy between us, a closeness beyond imagining, but the rest of the time our separateness is absolute. Such schizophrenia could bring even those with the strongest equilibrium to the edge of reason, and let's admit it, I didn't have much equilibrium to begin with.

There is the insanity of not being able to be seen together. An insanity that is aggravated in this case by the unprecedented situation of finding ourselves in the middle of a crowd and having to act like strangers. It seems crazy not to be able to show our happiness. Such an impoverished word. Others have this right, and they exercise it freely. Sharing their happiness makes them even more happy, makes them expand with joy. But we're left stunted, compromised, by the burden of having to always lie and censor ourselves.

This passion that can't be talked about, that has to be concealed, gives way to the terrible question: if it isn't talked about, how can one know that it really exists? One day, when it's over, when it finally comes to an end, no one will be able to attest to what took place. One of the protagonists (Thomas) will be able to go so far as to deny it if he wants to, to insist that such nonsense was invented. The other (me) will have nothing but my word, which doesn't carry a lot of weight. And besides, that word will never come. I will almost never speak of it.

*　　*　　*

We are there at the party when suddenly, a young girl throws herself at him. She has emerged from the shadows, as if drawn to his light. She's putting a lot of energy and exuberance into flirting with him. The sight wounds me because her gestures don't seem impulsive, they just seem natural. Thomas seems a little surprised, maybe even disconcerted, but he lets it happen, accepting her familiar affection. He gives her a kiss. While I could perhaps see it as the feminine version of the camaraderie I observed earlier, the jealousy that invades and overwhelms me makes me perceive the scene quite differently.

Jealousy, though not an entirely unknown feeling, is nevertheless somewhat foreign to me. I'm not possessive, figuring no one should have exclusive rights to someone else, as if a lover were a piece of property. I respect everyone's freedom too much (probably because I can't bear to have mine undermined). It seems to me that I am capable of good judgment, even detachment. These are qualities that have been attributed to me, even at that age.

Besides, I have always found the spectacle of "the tease" in either sex to be tiresome, it never made me envious. Except all my beautiful principles crumble in a second, the second this young woman throws herself at Thomas.

Because this scene not only shows a life lived outside of me. It hurtles me back to a void, to nonexistence, really, in the cruelest way.

Because it shows what is usually hidden from me.

Because it shows the charm of this mysterious boy and how many attempts must be made before one can get close to him.

Because it offers an alternative to Thomas the disoriented one who feels torn in different directions.

I cannot stand the idea that he could be taken from me. That I could lose him. I discover for the first time—poor idiot—this stabbing pain of love.

(And when you've been hurt once, you're afraid to try again later, in dread of enduring the same pain. You avoid getting hurt in an attempt to avoid suffering: for years, this principle will serve as my holy sacrament. So many lost years.)

Right after the hug, Thomas turns in my direction (one must not see here any cause and effect, no expression of the unconscious; it's only chance, his movements are slow), and his gaze finally lands on me. Never have I seen such a strike of lightning before. Yes, that's exactly it: it's as if a lightning bolt strikes him. First because my presence has been revealed. Then, I presume, because of the picture he is presenting at this moment, that of the boy seduced, having casually placed his hand on the girl's hip. Hard to do worse. He has the paleness and rigidity of a corpse. The girl doesn't notice anything, she continues smiling coyly, and shouting things in his ear because of the loud music and also no doubt to accentuate their closeness. He's no longer paying attention but she doesn't realize it. Only the friend next to him seems intrigued by the change in his facial expression, in the position of his body. But the friend doesn't deduce anything, it seems, since he does not look at me. He doesn't understand that I'm responsible for this transformation.

And what do I look like? I must not look much better. The pain must disfigure me, adding a mixture of spite and sadness to my expression. Nadine comes back holding two cups of punch. She sees everything, knowing me too well. Years later, she'll confide in me that she understood everything that night. Seeing my discomfort, she understood the love I carried for the dark-eyed boy and understood, too, my general love for boys. She had this revelation there, or rather the confirmation of it. As if she'd known before that moment, but the knowledge hadn't yet reached her consciousness. There, in the dim light of a birthday party, it became clear to her. At the time, she says nothing. She hands me a plastic cup. I take it as if in slow motion.

I drink an inordinate amount of alcohol, throwing back

the punch all night. I keep going back to serve myself from a large bowl with ragged pieces of blood oranges floating in it.

I talk to strangers, asking questions, pretending to be interested in them, and maybe I really am interested in them. It's just another way of not thinking about Thomas. The next day, some will go so far as to say that I'm a nice guy, *so much better than his reputation.*

I dance too even though I still don't know how to dance. I'm ashamed of my body and its weakness. But so what, we dance on volcanos, as the expression says. And anyway it's not fear of ridicule that's killing me.

I go out into the garden, hang out on the lawn. Some guys are smoking cigarettes in a corner and I ask them if I can have a drag. They laugh at my drunkenness but offer me one and I immediately start coughing. I'm definitely no good at it.

I ask where the bathroom is and I rush in and vomit. I stay in there for a long time with my head bent over the toilet. There's knocking on the door.

I get back on track. I dance again, forgetting my body, forgetting my humiliation.

Thomas and I avoid each other.

I say to myself: Basically, what's new? Don't we already spend most of our time avoiding each other? Missing each other? I smile at the double meaning—an unsightly, tragic smile, of course.

*　　*　　*

Later in the night, I'm seized by the desire to kiss him, to break from the crowd and go to him. Alcohol has lifted all my inhibitions. All except this one. Even in my current state of abandon I remain obedient to him, aware of the mortal risk I'd run. I decide to leave the party.

After, I remember walking home for a long time on the edge of the road in the cold, coming at last to the depressing gleam of the lampposts that signal the entrance to the city and twisting my ankle in a crack in the pavement. A dog barked, waking my parents. (The light went on in their room upstairs. They must have looked at the clock and whispered to each other.) I collapsed on my bed without even undressing. I had the time to think all the way home about how affairs of the body are so much more preferable to affairs of the heart, but that sometimes you don't have the choice.

When I see Thomas, two days later, I vow not to mention this evening, this shipwreck. He too doesn't say a word on the subject. We make love. It seems to me that there is a little more tenderness than usual. However, when our bodies are lying next to each other, eyes turned to the ceiling, the words we were not supposed to say all spill out. They are the cause of our first crisis. My jealousy erupts. My childishness. The explanation is stormy and awkward. Thomas lets me speak. At the end, he says: It's like that, there's nothing to discuss (to negotiate, I think he even says). *If you prefer, we can stop.* Right now, immediately, if you can't stand it anymore. I say: No, I don't want to stop. The terror of losing him outweighs any other consideration.

The clandestine meetings resume as before. Kisses on the body. Love in my bedroom. Everything in this room that belongs only to us. Everything that is incommunicable to the rest of the world.

One time, only once, do we face the unthinkable. My mother comes home unexpectedly. She didn't feel well and asked her boss to leave the office early. She slips her key into the front door but we don't hear her from the attic. She enters the house, drops her purse and things, thinking she's alone, and is surprised to hear echoes of conversation emanating from my room, since no one was supposed to be there. Worried, she calls out my name, but there's no answer. We are in a postcoital daze. Since she doesn't get an answer, my mother heads upstairs, her worry intensifying with every creak of the stairs under her feet. We hear the creaking and freeze, petrified. What can we do? Do we jump out of bed, running the risk of convincing her that something isn't right and thus hastening her up the steps, or do we not move and get discovered like this, stretched out naked in bed? She repeats my name, and I understand that it's my mother who approaches, that she will be there any minute, on the other side of the door, one foot away from seeing her world collapse. She is about to push the door open, it's inevitable now (but why is she not afraid? Why doesn't she run?); I say: Yes, I'm here, working. She says: But you are not alone, I heard talking. I say: I'm with a friend, we have a class that was canceled, and we came here to prepare a presentation. She says: Ah, well, I won't bother you then. She doesn't dare to push open the door. In the end we are saved by my ability to invent plausible lies. Then she says: But if you want a snack, I'll fix you something (she still prepares snacks for her seventeen-year-old son). I say: Thanks, but it's okay. I add: How are you? Why did you come back so early? (Thomas scolds me with a furious whisper: *Why do you push it? She was leaving!* I tell him: It confirms that I haven't done anything wrong, that there is no "wolf," I know how lies need to be cloaked.) My mother describes her migraine to me and the accompanying chills, still through the door, and finally says: I must be coming down with something. And then she goes back downstairs. Later, when Thomas and I appear in the kitchen as well-groomed high school seniors, cleansed of our sins and above suspicion, she looks at us without guile. Thomas walks over to shake her hand, respectfully. That evening she says: He is well brought up, your friend.

During this winter—or maybe spring?—Jean-Marie Le Pen, the far-right politician, appears on *The Hour of Truth* for the first time. He enters the studio of Antenne 2 alongside François-Henri de Virieu, accompanied by Paul McCartney's "Live and Let Die," with the air of a man who has already won. The Olympic Games are held in Sarajevo, Yugoslavia, which still existed then. It is six republics, five nations, four languages, three religions, two alphabets, and one party: "the House of Flowers," as Tito, who now resides in a mausoleum in Belgrade, was fond of saying. The country has not yet been dismembered but its communism is already dying. Perrine Pelen wins two medals in skiing. I remember her short hair and baby face. David, "the boy in the bubble," dies at the age of twelve. The miners begin their strike in Britain. No one knows yet that it will last a year, claim several victims, and inspire the Clash's song "London Calling," that in the end the strikers will return to work without getting anything and that from then on Margaret Thatcher will own the labor movement. In France, hundreds of thousands of people march to defend Catholic schools. As the son of a secular school educator, I find my political conscience is awakening. Indira Gandhi orders the assault on the Golden Temple of Amritsar, sending tanks to the Sikh sanctuary, and will be murdered by a Sikh a few weeks later. And then there is AIDS, of course. AIDS, which will rob us of our innocence.

I wrote the word: love. I did consider using another one. It's a curious notion, love; difficult to identify and define. There are so many degrees and variations. I could have contented myself with saying that I was *smitten* (and it is true that Thomas knew how to make me weaken), or *infatuated* (he could conquer, flatter, even bewitch like no one else), or *obsessed* (he often provoked a mixture of bewilderment and excitement, turning everything upside down), or *seduced* (once he caught me in his net, there was no escaping), or *taken with* (I was stupidly joyful, I could heat up over nothing), or even *blinded* (anything that embarrassed me, I pushed to the side, minimizing his defects, putting his good qualities on a pedestal), or *disturbed* (no longer was I ever quite myself), which would have had less positive connotations. I could have explained it away as mere affection, having a "crush," an explanation vague enough to mean anything. But those would just have been words. The truth, the brutal truth, was that I was in love. Enough to use the right word.

All the same, I wondered if this could be a complete invention. As you already know, I invented stories all the time, with so much authenticity that people usually ended up believing me (sometimes even I was no longer able to disentangle the true from the false). Could I have made this story up from scratch? Could I have turned an erotic obsession into a passion? Yes, it's possible.

In June, we take our baccalaureate. In July, we read a list on the blackboard telling us that we passed. I'm happy, as one is in these moments. Thomas acts like a killjoy. He starts in on me: You never really thought you *wouldn't* pass, it's not like you were shaking in your boots as you looked for your name on the list, right? Even the passing with honors wasn't a surprise to you. I tell him that knowing it doesn't prevent happiness, that we can still savor the moment. I did not understand then that the bac was *the end of us.*

Or rather I absolutely refused to see it, remaining in a stubborn state of denial. I had ignored the weight of the terrible phrase expressed to me on that first day: "Because you will leave and we will stay." (In hindsight, I'm shocked by my attitude. Ever rational and pragmatic, how did I manage to sweep away the evidence, the undeniable certainty of the end?) I suppose I didn't want to be overcome by grief in advance.

Later I will do the same with death. I will behave as if life will just continue. I will talk to a friend the day before

87

he dies, imagining the future, even when he is emaciated, intubated, clearly on his deathbed. When I hear of his passing, it will always be a surprise to me.

Thomas, however, has forgotten nothing. Nothing has disappeared for him. It's why he scowls. I do not know what is hiding behind that pose. If I had to think about it, I would say: melancholy, sadness, perhaps the beginning of nostalgia, which he will quickly excise; or nothing at all, since he has been so good at refusing to commit himself. In any case, I would not say: despair.

For me, when I finally realize the extent of the rupture, my heart will break. It is pure suffering. I always figured it would be me who would suffer the most. I even thought that I would be the only one. Sometimes there is a lack of discernment.

Just after I get the results of the bac, I say: Hey, I have to show you the camera my parents gave me. He jokes: Well, at least they weren't very worried if they got you a gift before they knew. I shrug my shoulders. He adds: And that's the only pretext you've found to go to your house, to fuck, to celebrate, what. . . ? I burst out laughing; I don't know that it's my last laugh with him. The house is empty, the room welcomes our intimacy. And then, without thinking, and without much hope either, I make a suggestion: We could go for a ride on your bike, in the countryside, to use my new Canon. To my surprise, Thomas agrees, without complaining. We leave immediately. The air is warm, the light almost blinding. We end up stopping in a wooded area that I like, away from everything. I start taking my first pictures. Thomas stands a little behind; I guess he's amused by my childish excitement. He goes to sit on a low wall of pale stones and pulls out a blade of grass to hold between his fingers. I turn around, discovering him in this position, and find him more beautiful than ever. Behind him is an oak tree surrounded by a yellow sky. I want to immortalize this moment, this moment of his beauty at the beginning of summer, but I sense that he will tell me no if I ask him. And I refuse to photograph him without his knowing. I approach slowly, already resigned to his refusal. Yet, almost despite myself, probably because the desire is too strong, I find myself asking him. I can see the hesitation in his eyes, but in the end he accepts. I'm stunned but I don't show it and I hurry to get what I want before he changes his mind. I take the picture. In it, he's wearing jeans, a plaid shirt with rolled-up sleeves. He has the blade of grass between his fingers and he's smiling, a slight, complicit smile, almost tender. This smile devastated me for a long time after, whenever I happened to look at this photograph. It upsets me even now as I write these lines and contemplate the image, resting on my desk, right next to my keyboard. Because now I know. I know that Thomas consented to this single picture only because he knew (had decided) that it was our last moment together. He smiled so that I could take his smile with me.

And then it was time for my departure for the island of Ré, just like every summer since childhood. The island had always been a part of my life. The reason? My father's best friend, whom he'd met at twenty, during his military service, "in the regiment," as they say, lived there. When I search my memory, the oldest one I can think of is on the island: I'm three years old, wearing short pants, a striped shirt, and a miniature bicycle cap, sitting on my mother's lap in front of a boat. The sun makes me squint. The boat is the ferry that connects the mainland to the island, between La Pallice and Sablanceaux. The crossing is twenty minutes long. The wonder I felt at this moment has never left me.

I spent every summer on the island. We would wait for hours in unbearable heat in a line at the pier, the leatherette of the car seats sticking to our bare thighs. Once we were on board the ferry, though, everything—the waiting, the humidity—would be forgotten. We'd get out of the car and let the euphoria wash over us. The smell of fuel and sea salt mingling together as we looked out over the flickering light on the surface of the water. When we arrived on the other side, we headed to Sainte-Marie.

*   *   *

The island is popular at that time: There are campsites, paid holiday vacations, Paul Ricard bucket hats, and folding tables on the sides of roads. It is not the extension of Saint-Germain-des-Prés that it has since become. The stone façades are dark, the shutters bottle green. In the afternoons, we head out to the other side of Saint-Sauveur on foot to go swimming. The roads are dotted with umbrella pines. I adore this beach, with its warm and turbid seawater that smells like kelp. In fact, I almost drowned here once (which, who knows, might be responsible for my obsession with drowning so many characters in my novels—and yet the experience itself left me with no lasting consequences).

Today, when I meet children on this beach, when I see them running in the dunes, or lying on the hot stone wall that was once a levee, I remember that I was like them once, with their incredible lightness and insouciance, soaking in the sun. You can never really let go of your childhood. Especially when it was happy.

(I will sometimes lament that my childhood and my adolescence were so protected, so ordinary and indolent, because one is so often expected to recount a childhood trauma to justify being a writer. But for me there was no crazy family, no abuse, no father who was absent or particularly present, no running away or drifting. No serious illness, no poverty, and no great wealth either—nothing really to make a book that catches the eye.)

In short, this summer of 1984 should not have been any different. There is always the large bay of Rivedoux, the small cliffs of La Flotte, the flat beaches of Bois-Plage, the marshes of Ars, the rocky point of Saint-Clément. The hollyhocks in alleys, pine needles crunching underfoot in the forest of Trousse-Chemise, the green oaks under which one goes to find shade. The fortifications of Vauban to protect me from imaginary invasions, the open-air abbey that always terrified me at night, and the Whales lighthouse, whose spinning light makes me dizzy. Always the same boys my age; before we went to the carousel, now we go to the bar. Everything is in its place, everything reassures me. Except that I miss Thomas. I miss him terribly. And that changes everything. Have you noticed how the most beautiful landscapes lose their brilliance as soon as our thoughts prevent us from seeing them properly?

I do not write a letter, let alone a postcard; he forbade it. I phone very little, as he strongly advised me. Anyway, during the day he works in the fields and is unreachable. In the evening, I don't know what he's doing. I don't want to know. Then, as is his tradition, he goes to Spain and becomes inaccessible for good.

At the beginning of August, I sleep with a boy who set up his tent at the Grenettes campsite. We have sex under the canvas, indiscriminately, on a blanket stinking of sweat. I went with him because of his blond hair, bleached out by the sun and salt, his golden skin and green eyes, and because it was easy. I wasn't looking for a diversion, or a way to soothe my pain. I wasn't looking for an alternative. I just gave in to the ease of it. That was all.

I am taken aback by this other body, so different from Thomas's. I can't find my bearings and it's disconcerting. But it's nice, too. When I return to Barbezieux around the fifteenth of August, I call Thomas but get his sister Nathalie (the secretary) instead. She tells me in a monotone voice: He stayed in Spain. I don't know if you know, but we have family there. (She uses the formal *"vous"* with me since she doesn't know me. Her tone is offhanded. I imagine that she's busy doing something else: putting on nail polish or brushing her hair.) She goes on: They offered him a job, and he said yes, since he didn't want to continue his studies. There's a noise in my head as she finishes saying these words. It's the sound of a ship's horn as it casts away from the mainland. I don't know why.

One day, I will find myself writing about ships leaving. I will write the story of a woman who waits on the quay in the port of Livorno watching the ships go. I will always remember the flat prolonged sound of the ship's horn blowing in my ear as the summer of 1984 ended. A roar that gradually dies out, little by little.

After, it's something else. It's no longer a noise, but rather a physical sensation, a shock, like a collision. Like a casualty that the paramedics extract from a pile of mangled sheet metal and immediately put on a stretcher, throw in the back of an ambulance, and leave in the hospital emergency room entrusted to the care of the doctor on call. The wounded who's operated on urgently because of blood loss, broken limbs, and other injuries. The stitched-up, bandaged survivor who wakes up slowly from the anesthesia, still groggy under the effects of the chloroform, already caught up by the pain that comes back to him, the memory of the trauma. And then the disoriented convalescent without energy, without will, who asks himself if it would've just been better if his body had been left to die in the crash but who eventually heals, because as is often the case, you eventually heal.

*   *   *

Yes, it's this hackneyed analogy that is the most apt.

At the beginning of September, I leave Barbezieux. I go to college at the Lycée Michel-de-Montaigne in Bordeaux, working toward a graduate degree in business. I begin a new life, the one that was chosen for me, bowing to the hope and ambition that have been placed in me.

I erase Thomas Andrieu.

Chapter Two
2007

More than twenty years have passed. Bordeaux has completely transformed from the dark, soot-covered town I knew at eighteen. Since the buildings were cleaned, the ocher color of the façades dominates, bringing lightness to a city that was oppressive in its decline. There were abandoned slaughterhouses, tall grass, barbed wire, mud—you can't even imagine. The bourgeois population was aging; now it is young, bohemian. Since the youth now predominates, the evenings in town have taken on a Spanish flair. You can see it in the happy faces of the people congregating in the squares, chatting on the café terraces, their tinkling glasses and bright conversations floating on the wind. Most of all, the city has rediscovered the river. The banks and quays have all been renovated. With the manicured lawns and rows of plane trees—the vast Miroir d'Eau reflecting pool with the sleek and modern tram running beside it—the city has been restored to its former elegance.

I became a writer. I've come to a bookstore here in Bordeaux for a reading of my latest novel. It will be too late to return to Paris afterward since all the trains will have stopped running, so I've booked a hotel room not far from the Allées of Tourny. The next morning, I have to meet a journalist and then I hope to enjoy the city a little, perhaps walk along the banks of the Garonne River before returning home. It is that morning, just as the interview is coming to an end, when I see the silhouette, the back of the young man with his suitcase leaving the hotel.

I see *this image that cannot exist* and cry out the name. Rushing to catch the boy on the sidewalk, I put my hand on his shoulder, and he turns around.

It's almost him.

The resemblance is uncanny. So much so that it sends a tremor down my spine. I feel short of breath and lose my balance for a moment. (This kind of situation actually can cause a physical reaction. The body responds as if it's in imminent danger: the muscles contract, the limbs suddenly go limp.) The boy's features are the same, the look is the same—it's alarming. Crazy-making. But there is a tiny difference, something in the smile, or maybe just his overall demeanor. It's this tiny difference that manages to bring me back to reason. I don't say to the young man: Sorry, I was wrong, I thought I recognized someone. Nor do I say: If you knew how much you resemble someone I haven't seen for a long time . . . Instead I say: You are the spitting image of your father.

He responds immediately: People tell me that all the time.

And then there is nothing more to say. I continue to gaze at him as one would a painting. I linger on every feature, scrutinizing him almost as though he weren't alive, as if he weren't right there looking back at me.

My body begins to calm down.

The young man has every right to be embarrassed by this inspection and try to put an end to it, to find it out of place, even rude. But he chooses instead to have fun with it. He smiles. I was right; the smile is not exactly the same.

I ask if he's in a hurry, or if maybe he has time for a coffee. The question arises without prior reflection, without the filter of intelligence. It testifies to my need to keep this "miracle child" near me; to question him more thoroughly, to fill a twenty-three-year-old gap. I don't have time to counter this urge, let alone to decipher or be troubled by it. He says that his train is not for another hour, that he can stay for a bit. Immediately (paradoxically), I am shocked that he could so easily accept the solicitation of a stranger: I wouldn't have. I would have refused to submit to such an interrogation and gone on my way, glad to be alone.

He has understood, of course. He knows what accounts for my interest in him, but why would that be enough for him to stay? Especially since, as he said himself, people frequently make the comparison to his father; he should be tired of it by now. But he doesn't say he's tired of it, he just keeps smiling. And then he gives an explanation for accepting my invitation.

He says: *You must have liked him a lot, to look at me like that.*

*   *   *

We go back into the hotel, where I abruptly end my interview with the journalist, and we sit down at the same table.

I say: I don't even know your name.

He says: Lucas (and I'm disturbed by this name, since I have so often used it in my books—as if there were no such thing as chance). I don't give him my name, and he doesn't ask.

He goes on: So you are an old friend of my father's, is that it?

I hear the description, finding it lovely, false but lovely. I say: Yes . . . that's it, an old friend . . .

I stop speaking. The words are stuck because the emotion has come back. It's the voice and the resemblance. The gestures, too, which are fascinating in their similarities. It makes me wonder about the part nature plays versus nurture.

I ask him if Thomas is well. (I don't say Thomas. I say, "your father.") The question has the appearance of being a polite one, a natural beginning to a conversation, but it's something else, something more existential. Fortunately, the young man doesn't detect anything, he hears only politeness. The smile returns to his face, but I notice confusion and perhaps even a touch of bitterness mingled in it.

He says: It's always so difficult with him to know how he is. He's always so withdrawn . . . Was he already like that, in your day?

I know "in your day" is intended without malice, but it still manages to put my youth firmly in the past, turning it into a sort of curiosity. I answer that indeed I never knew his father to be extroverted, that he often withdrew into silence, or at least the background. Lucas seems very different: playful, open, not at all antisocial. It seems that part was not inherited.

I ask if Thomas still lives in the same place, surprising myself by my indiscretion. The son confirms: Obviously! Could you see him living anywhere else? My father is one of those guys who'll never leave, who will die where they were born.

By reflex I say: And not you?

He nods his head: I want to go somewhere else. It's normal at my age, right?

I agree, without insisting. I point out that his father also went away one day, since he found a job in Spain. I add: It was then that we lost touch, he and I. These last words are articulated with the least possible affect, as if life is just like that sometimes, you spend time together and then lose touch and life goes on—as if there were no breaks from which you never quite recover.

The son takes issue: Galicia is not exactly Peru! It's just next door. And then: It's family for us. Frankly, there are far more impressive exiles.

I sense the ambition and ease of a generation that has grown up on a much smaller planet. Those who consider travel an ordinary adventure rather than a grand expedition, for whom a quiet life is considered a slow death. I see this child of the world and can't help but think how fate probably would have played out differently had his father been driven by the same curiosity. If he had not lived in another day. If he had known how to free himself.

The boy adds: Well, having said that, without his Spanish digression (digression: could we find a more apt term?), I never would have been born. At my obvious confusion, he immediately clarifies: He met my mother there.

And so the story unfurls:

Thomas works on a large property in Galicia with his uncles and cousins. It is said that he works hard, that he puts all his strength into it, and refuses no task, even under the burning sun or heavy rain. He begins early in the morning and is one of the last to finish, leaving the other men in awe of him. His aunt says that he is obsessed with work. Could she have guessed that it wasn't quite normal for a young man of eighteen years old, one who could have continued his schooling, to throw himself into chores that required only his arms, his brute strength? Did she perceive that this self-lessness was probably a way of forgetting himself, of putting himself to the test, maybe even of hurting himself? (It's me who thinks that. Lucas is content to evoke the heroic image of a boy plowing the earth under inhuman conditions.)

One evening Thomas is at a party in a village that is festooned in flags. At the sound of a drunken accordion he turns and sees a young girl. She is seventeen years old, with dark hair and olive skin, and her name is Luisa. He walks toward her. (Here, I believe the story must have been rewritten. The scene cannot possibly be so cinematic. The years spent telling and retelling it have surely shaped it into a kind of family legend.) I'm guessing that there was probably no bolt of lightning, just a warm night full of wine and fluttering moths and the feeling that nothing is really important and everything is possible. I'm sure that Thomas would not have gone naturally to the girl himself, that he would have been trapped by his reserve, and *by what he is*; it was she who had to have overcome her inhibitions. It was she who figured out how to manage his fear and shame. I also know how much of yourself you have to leave behind in order to look like everyone else. This is what is at play in the Galician night—the night of the flags.

*   *   *

This scenario could have been without a future. It should have been. I think of all the boys I met for a few hours after a night of drinking or drugs and never saw again. Those bodies entwined over warm nights and lost in the early morning. Eyes that caught mine and were forgotten as soon as pleasure came. I have been a moment of passage for these boys too, an ephemeral lover, without a name—how many really remember me? Normally youth is like that, without attachments, without obligations. Yet these two particular young people see each other again and become closer. I am sure that Thomas compels himself to.

I know that there are those who will object to my refusal to accept that he changed course, switched orientation, simply succumbed to a feeling that was previously unknown to him. I could be seen as upset, jealous, or even obtuse, and yet I persist in thinking that he put the same stubborn application into this as he did to his work. The same desire to forget himself, to return to the righteous path set out by his mother, the only one permissible. Does he end up believing it himself? That's the fundamental question. If the answer is yes, then moving forward in life would be possible. If the answer is no, then it is a life condemned to interminable misery.

And then an accident (let's call it that) decides things for them—for him. Luisa becomes pregnant. Bad luck, clumsiness, carelessness, it doesn't matter, a child is coming. A child who will grow in his mother's womb, one who cannot be done away with—it's Catholic Spain after all, you don't mess around with these kinds of things.

It is "the accident" himself who explains it this way. He knows that he was unwanted, that he was conceived when his parents were young and barely knew each other, that their roads would probably have diverged had there not been this "accident." He knows that in another time, another country, another culture, he would never have come into the world. He says: But hey, that's the way it is. He adds: And anyway, I believe that children who were not wanted don't necessarily grow up worse off than the others. He's not wrong. I too was an unwanted child, an accident. My mother was twenty when she gave birth to me and I never felt that I wanted for love.

When she learns of the pregnancy, Thomas's mother—usually so mild-mannered and reserved—insists upon a wedding. It takes place two months later, in the church of Vilalba. You don't go against the will of a woman who has expressed so little in her life. And where is Thomas in this story? He doesn't refuse, of that I am certain. It's not possible. They are all too powerful, telling him what he *has to do* as they oversee him. But he probably doesn't want to rebel either. They are so happy! His father, who sighs in relief that his son will not leave the land; his mother, who is delighted that her son, twenty years later, is following the same story of a Frenchman marrying a young Spanish girl. Everything has fallen into place. Thomas lets it happen, resigning himself to fate. Perhaps he also tells himself that it's a sign, that circumstances have given him the chance to escape from a life of deviance, and that now everything can return to order.

The wedding is celebrated in the spring.

Lucas says: I've seen the wedding pictures, my mother put them in an album. She looks at them regularly, she must like to remember her youth. (Or else she confuses youth with happiness, as people frequently do.) In these shots taken over twenty years ago, the teenage bride and groom stand awkwardly on the steps of the church in borrowed finery, showered with grains of rice, surrounded by family.

In other images, the newlyweds are in a garden. The bride clasps a bouquet in her hands under an archway of cascading wisteria; the groom stands beside her, with a straight neck. At the evening dinner, with everyone sitting at a long communal table, there is a feeling of togetherness. The married couple take their first steps under a garland of flowers exploding with color. The stone walls of the farm, the strangely Celtic landscapes, offer a deceptive image of a hopeful, open-ended future.

*　　*　　*

Lucas adds: Even so, there is something that has always struck me in the photos . . . my father often looks sad. I guess he didn't like having to smile on command.

It's clear to me that the sadness was unrelated to the demands of an overzealous wedding photographer, but of course I stop myself from saying anything.

I think: If it was already there, this sadness, from the very first hours of the marriage, if it was so massive that it could not be concealed even then, during these moments of the greatest communion, during the happiest of feasts—how heavy must this weight have become in the years that followed?

The young man continues: I understand why people say that I look like him. In the photos, I have the same impression that I'm looking at myself, except of course, I smile.

I remember one day finding a photo-booth strip, forgotten on a bookshelf of the den in the house in Barbezieux, and wondering: when was this photo taken? I searched for a date, or a theory that could have told me the age I might have been. I figured I must have needed a photo for my identity card, and since there is never a need for every picture from these sets of four, these must have been leftover ones, the ones that turn up in a drawer or a wallet years later. I showed the strip to my mother, who looked at it, saying in an offhanded way: It's not you, it's your brother, don't you recognize his sweater? It took me a few minutes to recover from having accepted a version of myself with someone else's face. As if I were only a copy.

Lucas tells me that he doesn't understand how you can take everything from one of your parents and nothing from the other. I suggest that maybe his brothers and sisters, if he has any, look more like their mother, that the distribution of features may have worked out like that. He specifies that he is an only child, that there were no children after him. His mother wanted one but his father refused. He never gave in, though this did not stop his mother from complaining, sometimes in front of others, which brought a flash of anger to his father's eyes.

He whispers (yes, he really speaks lower. His voice is choked as if he were confessing a secret) that he would have liked to have had a little sister, that he would have felt far less alone in childhood. He describes the loneliness of the farm, with the fields stretching out as far as the eye can see and only adults around him. He corrects himself. His father's sister was sometimes like a little sister to him, because you had to take care of her all the time, she was not independent, and looking after her was a way to feel useful. Living by her side was like living in a fairy tale because she had these moments of pure poetry—she invented whole worlds. He tells me that eventually she was placed in a specialized institution, that in the end his father resigned himself to it: the death of his soul. She is still there.

I assume that Thomas returned to France to work with his father. Lucas says yes, that's what happened. His youth was over. No more Spain. There was Charente, the wife, the son to raise, the sister, the vineyard, the herd.

I ask him if he still looks like his father today. He says: Oh yes! He hasn't changed, you know. It's almost strange to change so little, to age so slowly. If you saw him, you'd recognize him right away.

I'm reassured by this vision of an undiminished Thomas, whom the years have not weighed down or damaged. I know so many men who collapse around their thirties. I am one of such men. The hair thins, the features thicken; there are few who are immune to it. I'm no longer the lean teenager in a high school courtyard on a winter morning. The hair is cut short, the face plainly transfigured by time. The overall appearance has become somewhat urbane. Only the myopia has remained. I still wear glasses.

I'm also disturbed by the prospect, brought up by the son so casually, of seeing his father again. I never considered such a possibility. Very quickly, at eighteen, after I learned

111

that he had settled in Spain and I began my own new life, I had to admit to myself that what we had lived through together belonged irrevocably to the past.

His "if you saw him" can never be realized. It is out of the question.

(I correct myself because I've just been lying. Of course, it took time, a lot of time, before I admitted that everything was lost, before I decided to say goodbye forever. I kept hoping for a sign. I thought of initiating another meeting, I started letters that I never sent. Desire does not go out like a match, it extinguishes slowly as it burns into ash. In the end I gave up on all possibility of a reunion.)

Lucas glances at his watch and I notice that he's wearing Thomas's digital Casio. He catches my surprise, without knowing what it is connected to (the image of his father lying naked next to me in bed a quarter century ago). He thinks that it's *vintage*, one of those old things that have come back into style. He shakes his wrist and says: I have to go now. If I don't, I'll miss my train.

But I'm not ready to lose this accidental child. Not yet, not like that. Instead, I propose that I accompany him to the train station. I say: Why don't we take a taxi? It'll be much faster. He accepts my invitation without hesitating.

(In my panic, is there a part that is desire? An almost identical Thomas having been put in front of me, would it be so surprising if an identical desire reemerged?)

We walk to the Grand Theater, find a taxi, and head down the rue Esprit des Lois near the Place des Quinconces, then drive along the quay and pass in front of the Place de la Bourse. The building's stone façade glows yellow in the morning sun, and the reflection in its high windows almost blinds us. There is a stretch along the Garonne where I can't help but think of all the young men who've drowned there, without explanation, missing boys found weeks later. Those about whom it was never determined whether they jumped off a bridge or slipped accidentally from the wharf or were thrown violently into the water. We pass near the Saint-Michel district, where I spent time as a student of the Lycée Montaigne. The memories rush back—I see myself staggering home in the early morning, aware that I could have been one of those boys who drowned.

We take a detour onto one of the darker streets, one that hasn't been modernized yet, and then get back onto the Canal Marne and then finally reach the Saint-Jean train station. The entrance looks nothing like the one I knew. Before it was dirty, windy and gloomy; today a gleaming tram glides silently along an esplanade.

*   *   *

During the drive to the train station, I say: I didn't even ask what you're doing here in Bordeaux. He explains that he's only here in passing. He came to interview for an internship at a vineyard in the Médoc region. Since the interview was scheduled for late yesterday, he had to stay the night. Now he's going back to Nantes, where he's studying. I say: So you want to work in wine? He laughs and says no, what he wants is to work in exports.

We enter into the din of the station. I recognize the pink and brown marble walls, the staircase in the middle of the hall. I think perhaps I should have said goodbye in the taxi. I was surprised by his insistence that I accompany him to the platform and yet I gave in easily. I ask him if the train he is waiting for is still a Corail. He says it is. It's the same train that I would take on Friday nights returning home from Bordeaux on the weekends. I remember the sliding doors and the accordion passages between the cars. The clamor of moving from one car to another, and the stench of the toilets, that terrible mixture of urine and wholesale disinfectant. The long narrow corridors of the carriages where eight people could sit. People smoking, soldiers in uniform on a two-day leave from their garrison, with their khaki satchels and uninhibited manhood. I remember how long the trip seemed to me. It wasn't, but since we stopped at all the stations, it seemed endless.

To alleviate the boredom, I read, devouring the books of Duras and Guibert as I sat in my seat, among the young soldiers.

I got off at Jonzac, the nearest station to Barbezieux (there was no station in Barbezieux—apparently the town didn't want it), and my mother waited for me in the car, in the parking lot. She didn't know about the Guibert and the young soldiers. Or rather, she pretended not to know and we didn't talk about it.

I believe that Lucas will get off at Jonzac. Or maybe Châtelaillon-Plage, a quaint resort town where I happen to own a house, a seaside villa bought on a whim that ended up becoming the inspiration for one of my novels.

He couldn't possibly know where my thoughts have led me, yet he suddenly throws out: By the way, you didn't tell me whether you're working on a new book right now . . .

I stare at him, dumbfounded. Amid the pink and brown marble, in the chaos of the comings and goings, it's as though he were suddenly revealed to me, as though everything I thought I knew about him was wrong. I found him then to be completely devoid of ingenuousness, of the innocence that had suited him so well.

The image is that of two men suspended in the middle of a moving crowd.

I say: You know that I write?

He says, Yeah, I know who you are. I knew who you were the minute I saw you on the sidewalk in front of the hotel.

*　　*　　*

He expresses himself with confidence but without boast-
ing. At this point, I assume that he may have seen me once
on television and that he must just have an excellent memory. Perhaps he has read one of my books, but I doubt it;
twenty-year-old boys don't really read my books, or very
few of them anyway. Putting an end to my speculation he
says: My father told me about you. One day when you were
on TV, he said that you went to high school together.

He remembers how strange, even agitated, his father
seemed, and it surprised him because normally he had only
known his father to be calm. He put the agitation down to
surprise—it's not every day you see someone you know on
TV. It isn't every day a person emerges from your distant
past without warning.

I say, But how did you remember me? If you only saw me
the one time. He corrects me: No, I've seen you several
times. Whenever the TV guide says you're going to be on
a show, we watch you. His father insists on silence, while
his mother prefers to return to the kitchen. Writers don't
interest her much, nor does what her husband experienced
before knowing her. The son stays with him but doesn't
dare ask questions. He suspected that his father would not
have answered them anyway (a trait I recognize well). The

first time it happened he remembers paying more attention to his father, whose eyes were fixed on the television screen, than to the show itself.

He says: Though my father never reads books, he's read yours. He intimates that the books are in their house, though not in plain sight; no doubt they're tucked away in a closet somewhere or in the attic. In any case, he knows they are there. He remembers a cover: A painting, a bar, a woman in a red dress sitting at the counter, a man next to her wearing a suit and a hat. They stand very close to each other, almost touching. There is something between them, but it is hard to tell whether the intimacy is just from the physical proximity. There's a waiter on the other side of the counter, dressed in white, leaning forward, busy with who knows what. He says, It's an American painting, right? I tell him the name of the painter, Edward Hopper, but I cannot articulate another word.

The tumultuous comings and goings of the travelers, all these lives intersecting, bodies brushing against each other before disappearing forever, like in the hotel lobby, and the ads on the speaker punctuated by this horrible jangling sound—this *tatatala* noise—exasperate me. It feels like Lucas is disappearing; even the scenery is becoming blurry, like the melting watches of Dalí. The boy's voice brings me back: So? What are you working on right now? It takes me a few moments before I reply. First, I say that I don't know how to talk about a book while it's being written because it's still in flux, too vague, and because I am not certain of going to full term (I deliberately use this expression, borrowed from the vocabulary of childbirth). I add that it's also superstition on my part. I understand by his expression, the raised eyebrows, that he doesn't believe a word I'm saying. I give in and say: The story of two inseparable friends who end up being separated by time. He smiles. I urge him not to read anything personal into it. I specify that my books are fiction, that memoir doesn't interest me.

He asks if I have a title yet, because they are important, titles. I answer that I'm not sure yet, but he insists. I tell him that the novel will probably be called *The Betrayal of Thomas Spencer*. He seems to consider whether or not this is a good title. I'm afraid he'll be jarred by the name of the hero and give me a knowing smile again. But no. He raises his head toward the departure board, as if to check whether his track number is displayed yet, and then returns his gaze to me. He says: So, your Thomas Spencer, he's betraying his friend, right? I say: It's a bit more complicated . . . In fact, it's his youth he betrays.

He says: It's the same thing, no?

Suddenly, his track number appears on the giant board. In the throng of people, he announces that he has to go now, that he would have liked to have talked more, but that he's very happy to have met me. He shakes my hand and then leaves. There is no emotion or ceremony. He just walks away. The parting takes less than ten seconds.

After a few steps, he stops and comes back to me and says: You have something to write with? I'll give you his number. Call him. I'm sure he'd like to hear from you.

I enter the ten numbers into the phone as he gives them to me. The ten numbers that make Thomas accessible to me for the first time in twenty-three years.

He looks at me for a long time afterward. I don't understand his insistence. I say: What? What's the matter?

He says, What's your number? I'm asking because you're not the type to call.

He takes down my number. I say: And your father, do you think he's the type to call?

He stares at me again for a long time. Once again I'm confounded by the resemblance.

He says: That's for you to say. I'm sure you know him a lot better than I do.

And this time, the twin child goes away for good. And I feel a profound loneliness, the kind you feel when you are alone in the beating heart of a crowd. The only thing to do now is to leave the station. And to walk. To walk for a long time.

I will never call Thomas.

However, I will hesitate often. More than once, I will grab a phone and dial the numbers. I will only have the last key left to press and then each time, I will hang up.

The reasons? They will change according to the days. At the time, I live with a man who is fifteen years younger than me and doesn't like boys but loves me. Who knows why? It's a vulnerable relationship, and I will be scared to disturb this precarious equilibrium. Calling Thomas, talking to him, asking to see him again, would be anything but innocuous. I cannot say: This is only a phone call. I know it's more than that. Even if I were granted immunity, the act of calling him has the allure of betrayal (we come back to that, we always come back to it) or without going to that extreme, a gesture toward Thomas would be a gesture of mistrust toward the man I live with—a decision to put distance between us, to admit to a love that is not enough.

I also dread the cruelty of reality. We were eighteen— now we are forty. We are no longer who we once were. Time has passed, life has rolled over us and transformed us. We will not recognize one another. It doesn't matter how well appearances have been preserved, it's who we are, at the root. He is a married father who takes care of a farm in Charente. I am a novelist who spends six months of the year abroad. How could the circles of these two existences have even one point of intersection?

Above all, we will no longer find the thing that first pushed us toward one another that day. That singular moment. The pure urgency of it. There were circumstances—a series of coincidences and simultaneous desire. There was something in the atmosphere, something in the time and the place, that brought us together. And then everything broke—like a firework exploding on a dark night in July that spirals out in all directions, blazing brightly, dying before it touches the ground, so that no one gets burned. No one gets hurt.

Thomas will never call either.

Chapter Three
2016

A few weeks ago, I received a letter from Lucas, originally addressed to my publishing house, then forwarded to my home. He wrote to me nine years after our one and only meeting. In the letter, he said he would be in Paris during the last week of February (I noticed the letter was post-marked Charente) and that he would like to see me, in fact, he absolutely has to see me, because he has to give me something. He remained enigmatic, as if this enigma were necessary to get a favorable answer, or as if he were not sure that the letter would really come to me, and maintaining a certain mystery was necessary. He imagined that I was very busy, mentioning the title of my latest novel, but hoped that I could *find a moment* for him. He left a phone number, assuring me that he could adapt to my schedule since his was flexible.

I was on a book tour but mostly available during this last week of February and had no reason to decline his invitation.

And, I admit, I was intrigued.

I didn't dare call him. I was reluctant to start a conversation on the phone, thinking he would feel it necessary to fill me in on the intervening years and postpone entering directly into the heart of the matter. I thought that this kind of exchange would put us on shaky ground. I decided to send him a text proposing a time and a place. Less than a minute later, he replied: I'll be there.

I chose the Beaubourg café in the morning because it's near where I live and, on the second floor, it's calm. Almost no one ever goes up there. I also like the view onto the Pompidou museum.

I arrive first, a little nervous, and flip through the newspapers I purchased at the kiosk below without really reading anything in particular. I merely glance at the coverage of the American primaries and the photos of Donald Trump and Hillary Clinton accompanying the articles. This billion-dollar pre-election frenzy would ordinarily obsess me, but not this morning. Not on the morning of the reappearance of Lucas Andrieu.

When he appears, I recognize him immediately. He climbs the spiral staircase slowly, looking for me. As soon as he spots me, he walks in my direction. He is less the casual and carefree boy that I remember, the gracefulness of adolescence has faded. More solid and built, a man has come in his place.

There is no smile either. I remembered his radiance, his vitality. A kind of solemnity has taken over his features now. But perhaps it's only reserve, a little reticence for this reunion after all these years. A scheduled meeting absent of all chance can't help but take on an air of gravitas.

And yet what strikes me the most is his tanned complexion. I remark on it right away, which serves as a point of entry into the conversation, and like that, we manage to avoid the formulaic embarrassed greetings. He says: It's because I live in California now, it's sunny all the time there, as you know. He explains the "as you know," telling me that he came across an interview where I mentioned that I live part of the year in Los Angeles. He says: Sometimes I thought we would run into each other there. Of course LA is huge, I don't need to tell you that, endless even. But sometimes coincidences . . . Anyway, it never happened. And I couldn't call you because I didn't keep your number.

I ask what he's doing in California. He says that he works for a grand cru, one of those vineyards that buy French grapes and develop them on the spot. He tells me that he's the "sales manager," using the American term. I think to myself, At least someone realized his youthful ambition.

I say: And you returned to Charente to spend a few days of vacation? Immediately I notice a very quick but distinct shadow pass across his face. He begins to wring his hands, his eyes blink rapidly, and it's then that I understand that something has happened.

I understand that something terrible has happened.

He searches for the words but I don't want to hear them, as if one can refuse words that hurt as a horse refuses an obstacle.

Getting ahead of what he is about to tell me I say: When did it happen?

He says: Fifteen days ago. I came back as soon as I could.

He tells me about the shock of receiving the unexpected news, the call that came in the middle of the night because of the time difference, the sense of being suspended in limbo, the strange buzzing he had in his ears. He asked that they repeat it just to be sure he grasped what was being said, even though that was obviously useless; still, he needed to hear it again.

As he speaks, I go back to a Monday in May 2013. It was around nine thirty in the morning. I had turned my phone back on (I always keep it off at night) as I was getting ready to go to an appointment. I was on time (I'm always on time). Just as I was about to leave the apartment, my phone alerted me to a voicemail. I looked at the call list and saw that "Mom" had phoned me at 8:21 a.m.

I knew right away.

And yet, I had always imagined that it wouldn't happen like that. I had always assumed that I would pick up the phone on the day she called to tell me my father died. For months, my pulse would race every time I had to answer one of her calls. I had never considered that she would have to leave a message, that she would have no other choice.

Afterward, I thought she could have simply said: Call me back, and then have told me in person. But that would have been stupid, of course. Even the sound of her voice—

exhausted and wracked by sobs—would have been enough of a confirmation.

She said: It's Mom, it's over, Dad's gone. It's the most simple words that destroy us. Almost words for a child.

And after? After I called S., who was in the bathroom. I had to tell him twice: The first time I tried, barely any sound emerged. At the tone of my voice, he too immediately understood. He didn't ask any questions, but just came to hold me.

I was standing in front of the window, staring out over the treetops at the buildings on the rue Froidevaux, where we lived at the time, and he slipped behind me to hold me in an embrace. Then the tears came. I don't really know if I ended up saying anything. I don't think I did but I would have to ask S. His memory is so precise, he never forgets anything.

Lucas continues. In the aftermath, he had to take care of logistics—to return to Barbezieux, booking a ticket on the next flight from Los Angeles to Paris, and then another ticket for the train. He was lucky that there were still seats. (He smiles when he says "lucky.") He packed a suitcase, canceled his meetings, all the concrete and material things that distract us from grief, if only for a few moments. He did everything he could do to just hold on, one moment to the next, minute by minute, and on into the next day, when he finally reached his destination. Twenty-four hours later, he viewed his father's body in the mortuary.

When he pushes open the door upon which hangs a sign with the name of the deceased (this is how Thomas ends up, with his name on a door at the morgue), what strikes him the most is the bluish light and the smell of what he presumes to be the chemical used for embalming. It takes him a moment to look at the coffin, some last-minute bargaining with himself before giving in. When he finally brings his eyes to the open coffin, a sensation that he is unable to qualify takes hold of him: his father seems to be somewhere between life and death. The waxy stillness obviously proves he no longer belongs to the world of the living—not to mention the fact that he's lying in a coffin—but the makeup provides a strange sort of luminousness to his skin, which gives Lucas the impression that his father is only sleeping, that somehow his presence in the room might awaken him. He approaches carefully to touch his father's forehead. It's cold and hard, making his death undeniable at last. The only thing that Lucas finds reassuring is that the embalmers have done a remarkable job. You can't even see the trace of the rope around his neck.

He says: My father hung himself. We found him in his barn.

I would prefer not to visualize the scene, I would like to spare myself this masochistic impulse, but I can't help it. Even in these circumstances, it is the writer who wins. The writer who imagines everything; the one who needs to see it first to have it be seen. Against my will, the image forms in my mind. I see the body suspended at the end of the rope, the head bent, the compressed carotid artery. I see the rope hanging from a beam, gently swaying, with the chair turned over on its side, the rays of a winter sun filtering down through the planks and coming to rest in the bales of straw below.

A memory is superimposed onto this. It's the spring of 1977 or 1978—a teaching colleague of my father's was found hanged in her classroom. Her name was Françoise. I remember her great height, her long, unbrushed hair, the floor-length floral dresses she wore, the kind that were in fashion at the time. She must have been in her mid thirties. Some said that she killed herself to escape the stress of teaching. It's possible. In any case, everyone expressed their shock and sorrow. I was ten years old then and as inconceivable as it may seem, I explained to everyone that I was not surprised, that you could see the unhappiness on her. I said she had simply decided not to go on. At that age I knew nothing about death, let alone suicide, but that's the phrase that came to me. I was told to be quiet.

A confession: I do something else too. I ask myself: what did Thomas think about in those last moments, after having put the rope around his neck, before toppling the chair? Once he made the decision, how long did it last? A few seconds? A minute? But a minute is interminable under these circumstances, so how then did he fill the time? With what thoughts? And then I come back to my question. Did he close his eyes and revisit scenes from his past? From early childhood? His body stretched out like a cross in the fresh grass, face turned toward the blue of the sky, the feeling of the sun on his cheeks and his arms? His adolescence? A motorcycle ride with the wind pressing against his chest? Was he lost in the details of things he thought he'd forgotten? Did he scroll through faces and places, as if he could take them with him? (In the end, I am convinced he never considered changing his mind, that his determination never faltered, that no regret, if there even was any, weakened his will.) I try to imagine the last image that formed in his mind, plucked from his memory, not expecting to figure it out, but believing that if somehow I could discover it, I could renew our intimacy. I would once again be what no one else has been for him.

Lucas says: I guess I know what you're going to ask me, but no. He didn't leave any explanation. We didn't find a letter.

I presume that they looked for this letter, hoping that it would assuage their gnawing guilt at not having seen anything coming and keep them from facing the questions, from having to confront the mystery of this death alone. But the deceased did not grant them the grace of such a letter. He left without relieving them of their bad conscience. Did he want to punish them? Or did he simply hold on to this fundamental truth: that in the end, death is only a matter between you and yourself?

Obviously, the grieving child spends many sleepless nights. It's a lot to lose a father. Even harder when the death is so premature. But we enter into the realm of the infernal when the death has been chosen. So yes, all of it will turn and turn in his head. It will tear at his stomach. He will try to remember the last time he saw his father in an attempt to form some kind of interpretation, and he will be angry at himself for not having perceived his despair (because, finally, that's what it is, isn't it?). But he will always stumble on this stubborn reality: he doesn't know. His only certainty will be sorrow.

I ask him about his mother, who was inevitably affected by the tragedy. Lucas immediately lowers his head. His slumped posture is like an additional defeat.

He tells me that she was not present at the funeral. He adds, in a poor attempt at justification, or perhaps as a means of delay, that there was almost no one there anyway, that the ranks of the church were more than sparse. He says that his father ended up paying the price for his isolation.

I reply that his wife's failure to appear could not merely be a consequence of his isolation. Something must have happened.

He raises his head; the time has come for him to tell the

whole story; no doubt this is why he summoned me—so that the story could be told to a person able to hear it.

A few years ago (the exact date is not mentioned), Thomas Andrieu decided to radically change his life. This change took place overnight. There had been no warning signs, he did not give any notice, though he had organized everything in advance.

He brings his parents, his wife, and his son together in the big kitchen of the farm. He is serious, determined, not trembling or clearing his throat. The child recalls his being firmly resolved and a little soulless. What he remembers best is the quiet. The father has hardly said anything yet but it's as if everyone is waiting for an explosion. He stands up straight, announcing to everyone that *he is leaving*. Imagine the stupefaction, the incomprehension, the bewilderment, the anger that arises, the uncontrolled crying, the imploring of the mother and the wife, but he will have none of it. He commands silence. He says that he has not finished, that he still has things to announce.

He specifies that he will leave the house and the farm, that it's all finished for him, that his father will have to find someone else, an apprentice or a successor who will accept the work, and then to sell to whomever will buy it when the time for retirement comes. He adds that when he leaves the farm he is also renouncing all of his rights to the inheritance of the land, that it will no longer concern him.

He continues to speak without expression, in a monotone. He looks at the family together in front of him, but it's as if they don't register, as if they have disappeared—as if he were speaking to the fields, the wind, the clouds drifting through a towering sky beyond the kitchen window.

He says that he hired a lawyer for divorce proceedings, that he wants everything to be done according to the law. There will be official separation papers, so that nothing remains unresolved and so that his wife will be able to *rebuild her life* if she wishes, she will not be bound by anything. He declares that he is leaving her the money, the joint inheritance. He will carry nothing away with him.

The son does not see it as a gesture of generosity or disinterest but rather as a radical way of settling the accounts and letting go, of eradicating the past.

His father adds that now that his son has grown and his studies are coming to an end, he is out of the woods and can easily get a job. Opportunities are waiting for him, the world will open her arms, and he does not worry about him and wishes him the best. He is convinced that the best will happen. He says he did *his part of the job*. (The son has not forgotten this phrase. At the moment he tells me this he folds his arms across his body as though he's in pain.)

His father says he's going to move elsewhere but won't name the place. He does not want anyone to try to contact him. He'll disappear and that's it. He expresses no guilt, nor does he provide any explanation. (I believe he must have acted exactly the same way when he chose to hang himself.)

An hour later, he leaves.

In the meantime his wife will have tried to hold him back, clinging to him in tears, counting on her distress and desperation to make him waver. He does not flinch. Thomas's own father will have viciously insulted him, throwing in his face that he will no longer be his son. But he seems indifferent to this excommunication, the insult coming from a distance, as one spits bile. His mother will have tried to bring him to his senses, imploring him to be *reasonable*, and here he will object saying that he has been reasonable for too long—this is perhaps the only path he will open.

Lucas will not say anything. He stays in a corner as a spectator, observing this newly discovered determination in his father, a man showing him the face of someone completely unknown to him.

Already a distant stranger.

During the eight years that follow, Thomas demonstrates an exemplary rigor: There is not a word, not a call, not the slightest sign of contact. He changes his phone number, no one knows his new address. He never appears, and no one runs into him, even by chance. Sometimes they wonder if he's dead.

The family accepts his dictum. They have no choice. Nothing can be done against the will of one man. But in this small world, they sail, day by day, between resentment and sadness, questioning and anger, confusion and hate. They speculate on what could have become of him. Perhaps he returned to Spain, or travels under an assumed name, or else he simply settled in a remote corner somewhere and lives as a hermit. Yes, everyone agrees that he inevitably returned to his natural state of solitude. He becomes a bit of a legend.

And then over time, it dissipates, and fades, dispersing like pollen in the air at the return of spring. Lucas whispers: You get used to everything, even the defection of those you thought you were bound to forever.

I say: You speak of defection?

He stares at me. He says: It's true, you're a writer, words are important to you. And you're right, they are. For a long time, I tried to write down words about his disappearance. I found a lot. I even classified them in alphabetical order, if you want to know: "abandonment," "absence," "death," "departure," "dissolution," "erasure," "escape," "extinction," "flight," "loss," "retreat," "vanishing," "withdrawal,"—the other ones I forgot.

But the one that seems most appropriate to him—the one he prefers—is "defection." Usually, it's used in connection with spies who crossed the border, when our world was divided into two blocs during the cold war. He says: It makes me think of that Russian dancer, Nureyev, was it? You know, in the early sixties, when he crossed the barrier between the Soviet camp and the Western camp at the airport in Bourget. Lucas sees in Nureyev's gesture something dangerous and romantic, a manifestation of insubordination, an irrepressible desire for freedom. And a certain élan. There are evenings when he is pleased and reassured to think that this same impulse was behind his father's disappearance. In the word "defection," too, there is another idea: that his father missed him. And this possibility is absolutely necessary to him.

At first there was simply the offense of his father's having escaped his obligations. He left the straight path, broke the unwritten rules, upset the established order, played against his team, trampled the trust placed in him, offended his family, betrayed everyone.

And then the wound was accompanied by the inevitable pain and sorrow. His father was not there when they were counting on him. He left a void with questions no one could answer, an irreducible frustration, an emotional demand that no one could possibly meet.

I ask Lucas if he ever tried to track his father down. He says: In the beginning, no. He respected his father's decision, even if he didn't understand it and it made him suffer. He also found it incredibly insensitive to his mother. (I think there also could have been an element of wounded pride in this refusal.) He admits that after a while he thought of looking for him, even considering hiring a detective. The need to understand became more important, also the need to talk to him, because that kind of silence can drive you crazy.

He says: Finally, I gave up. He had his adult life to lead, his future to build. He didn't intend to be weighed down by the past and this sad family business.

Resentment took over, and time did the rest.

All the same, I wonder how one accepts having a father in this in-between place, this absence that is not death, this indefinite inaccessibility, this phantom existence. How can one resolve it for oneself and not be consumed regularly by the need to put an end to this pretense? The need to just not put up with the strangeness any longer—to alleviate this terrible, intolerable missing (we keep coming back to the word). No matter how much you want to respect someone's freedom (even when you consider it selfish), you still have your own pain, anger, and melancholy to contend with.

But I do not pose the question to the son left behind.

*   *   *

And then, one day, unbelievably, sometime last year, the father comes back. He moves to a farm in the area. His family hears the rumors of his return but nobody wants to see him. Neither his parents, who consider him dead, nor his ex-wife, who has since returned to Galicia and remarried.

Only his son decides to visit him, during one of his trips to France.

He says that his father had changed, aging almost to the point of unrecognizability. Yet to his surprise, his father invites him over. He asks if he wants something to drink, as if they had only just seen each other the day before, as if life as they had known it hadn't been obliterated in the blink of an eye followed by an eight-year blackout. The son sits at the table and contemplates this wrinkled and worn-out old man. He feels no compassion, no longer seeing a likeness, and wonders if their uncanny resemblance ever existed at all. The only thing he recognizes in his father is his unsociability.

The conversation begins but quickly dwindles into banalities and monosyllabic murmurs. Soon it is only the son who speaks, so he ends up asking the inevitable question. He asks for an explanation of the departure and of the return. The father does not respond or give any justification. He just remains silent. The son asks if, at the very least, he feels any regret. The man raises his head and looks at his son.

He says: No. I could regret it *if I had had a choice. But I did not have a choice.*

He does not say anything else.

I ask Lucas if he understands his father's words.

He answers yes, and then clarifies: *Now*, yes. He confirmed my suspicions.

I say: Your suspicions? My voice shakes slightly. He hears the tremor and looks at me, with the obvious intention of making me understand that we are talking about the same thing, that he *understands*.

He says: I think it started to formulate in my mind when I met you at the hotel in Bordeaux, but not when you called after me in the lobby thinking I was my father, not when you called his name and said that I looked like him. After all, you were not the first . . . No, it happened a few moments later when you looked at me and you were unable to speak. I understood at that moment that you loved him—that you had been in love with him. At the same moment, I recognized you, I knew who you were . . . I knew that you were gay . . . you say it on television when you're interviewed. You always answer without hesitation. When I arrived in Nantes that day, I went directly to a bookstore and looked for your books. I found *His Brother*, *A Boy from Italy*, and *How to Say Goodbye*. I took all three and read them immediately. These books only made me more sure. In *Goodbye*, you write letters to a man you loved. A man who left you and who never answers you, and you travel all the time trying to forget him.

I say: It's not *me* who writes to this man, it's a woman, my heroine.

He says: Who are you trying to convince? He continues: In *His Brother*, the hero is outright called Thomas Andrieu. Are you going to tell me that it's a coincidence? I stop protesting. To deny it would be to insult his intelligence. He drives home the point: And in *A Boy from Italy*, you tell the story of a double life, a man who can't choose between men and women. Your novels were like pieces of a puzzle. They were enough to assemble a picture that made sense.

He goes on: Eight days later, I went back to Lagarde to my parents' home. I waited to be alone with my father to tell him that I had met you. I suspected that it was better for my mother not to be around. You should have seen his face at that moment: it was an admission. He didn't say anything at first, he even pretended not to attach any importance to it, but it was too late. In that first moment, when he heard me say that I had seen you, he didn't move, but I swear he lost his balance. At that exact moment I was certain that he had been in love with you. That such a thing had existed—my father in love with a boy. I didn't need to ask him the question. I don't think I could have found the courage anyway. Afterward, I said to myself: Maybe it was just a phase. Okay, yes, it existed, but it ended. He moved on to something else—to a life, a woman, a child . . . that must happen often, these things. I told myself: when he saw you on TV, it brought back the memory, but it was just nostalgia. A secret from the past . . . everyone has secrets; besides, it's good to have things that belong only to you. It could have stayed there. It should have stayed there. Except that two days after our conversation, my father brought us together to announce he was leaving.

The revelation stuns me. It's as if I've received an electric shock, with the paralysis that follows.

He asks: You don't have anything to say?

There is no bluster, no accusation. I sense only curiosity and a desire to connect.

I answer: I don't know what to say . . . And there is nothing more genuine than my inadequacy in this moment. He is still waiting. Waiting for me to say something.

I pull myself together and start by pointing out that the departure of his father seemed very organized: the divorce lawyer, the renunciation of his inheritance. He must have already known his destination; he did not decide it on a whim. I add that a meeting between his son and me could have stirred up memories but was not of consequence, or at least not this kind of consequence. There was no reason for it to provoke such an upheaval.

He says that he agrees with me. He thought about it a lot and what he discovered after his father's death only reinforced what he'd imagined to be true. According to him, this news only precipitated a choice that his father had been considering for a long time. It put everything into stark relief. His father had been lying for too long, he had to come to terms with himself, and now there was an urgency to it. He adds: All the same, I often wondered if he might have gone to join you (the romance of that, the madness of that). Now I know he didn't.

I give him a questioning look.

He says: After his death, the house had to be emptied. It was done quickly, he possessed almost nothing. He lived in great frugality, he even refused the money that I offered him. But in the drawer of a wardrobe, tidy and carefully hidden, I found letters. After reading them, I was very surprised that he kept them. Even more that he didn't destroy them just before killing himself. I guess he wanted me to find them. I suppose they replaced the farewell letter he didn't write, the explanation he didn't give. First, there were the letters that were addressed to him. They all came from the same man, dated from a short time before his return to Charente. It's clear that the man was his lover (the son pronounces the word without wavering, without judgment) but that they did not live together. It's also clear that their relationship was secret. The man couldn't stand this deception. He writes that he wants to live with Thomas in broad daylight, that he does not want to go on hiding anymore, that it eats away at him like a disease, both the love and the silence. He gives Thomas an ultimatum, writing that if Thomas refuses to live with him, then he prefers to end the relationship. Lucas says the last letter was written the day before his father's return.

Thomas did not give in to the threat; perhaps he didn't give in to love either. He left before the breakup.

I think: *In the end, he remained hidden all his life. In spite of the great departure, the ambitious effort to forge a new existence, he fell back into all the same traps: shame, the impossibility of sharing a love that endures.*

I think of all the men I met in bookstores, men who confided in me about having lied for years and years, before finally resolving to leave everything to start all over again (they will recognize themselves if they read these lines). Thomas never found their courage.

I say "courage," but it may be something else. Those who have not taken this step, who have not come to terms with themselves, are not necessarily frightened, they are perhaps helpless, disoriented, lost as one is in the middle of a forest that's too dark or dense or vast.

The son continues his story. In the drawer there was another letter, enclosed in a sealed envelope, slightly yellowed, with no mention of a recipient. He didn't think it was anything at all, maybe an invoice or some kind of official document. He opened it with some apprehension, fearing that it could be a paper detailing his father's last wishes; just as he had imagined, Thomas was in fact the author of the letter.

He says: It's a letter that was written a long time ago

but never sent. It's addressed to you. It starts with your first name.

It dates from August 1984.

I stare at Lucas. The series of revelations causes a sound to reverberate in my ears, the kind of distorted humming noise that an amplifier makes when it's shorting out. To escape this sound, I say: Did you read it? He answers yes. He pulls the letter out of his jacket pocket and hands it to me. It's a little wrinkled, folded in two. He says: That's why I asked to see you, so I could give it to you.

He adds: I would prefer that you read it later, when I'm gone, because it's a story between him and you, just between the two of you.

I say okay and take the letter. I wonder if, rather, he fears my distress and wishes to spare me from having a witness.

After, there is silence. Long minutes of silence. Because there is nothing more to say, because everything has been said. Because now there is only the need to leave one another but we can't quite bring ourselves to do it. We would like to stay together a little longer, to hold back the moment, because we both know that it's the last time, that there will be no more.

I end up saying: What are you going to do now?

He says: I'm going back to California. I booked a ticket for Sunday morning. Home is there now. I have nothing here. No more ties . . .

There is more silence.

He is the one who speaks again: What about you? You will write about this story, won't you? You won't be able to stop yourself.

I repeat that I never write about my life, that I'm a novelist.

He smiles: Another one of your lies, right?

I smile back at him. Will you allow me to write about it?

He shrugs: I have nothing to forbid.

Finally, he gets up. Slowly I do the same. He shakes my hand and then leaves without another word. All the same, the gesture lasts a little longer than custom demands. There is no ambiguity, just an extra moment of pressure, somehow in keeping with the extraordinary singularity of what has occurred between us.

I watch him walk away, down the stairs, out of the café, and out of sight.

I sit down with Thomas's letter still folded in my left hand. I think it would be better not to read it, what good can it do? It will only hurt me. He wouldn't have wanted me to read it, otherwise he would have sent it. But then Lucas's conviction comes back to me: *I guess he wanted me to find them.*

So I unfold the paper and the written words appear. I hear the voice of Thomas, his voice in 1984, the voice of our youth.

Philippe, I'm going to Spain and I'm not coming back, at least not right away. You are going to Bordeaux and I know it will be only the first step in a long journey. I always knew you were made for somewhere else. Our paths are separating. I know you would have liked for things to be different, for me to say the words that would have reassured you, but I could not, and I never knew how to talk anyway. In the end, I tell myself that you understood. It was love, of course. And tomorrow, there will be a great emptiness. But we could not continue—you have your life waiting for you, and I will never change. I just wanted to write to tell you that I have been happy during these months together, that I have never been so happy, and that I already know I will never be so happy again.

About the Author

PHILIPPE BESSON is an author, screenwriter, and playwright. His first novel, *In the Absence of Men*, was awarded the Emmanuel Roblès Prize in 2001, and he is also the author of, among other books, *Late Autumn* (Grand Prize RTL-Lire), *A Boy from Italy*, and *The Atlantic House*. In 2017 he published *Lie With Me*, which has sold more than 120,000 copies and was awarded the Maison de la Presse Prize, and *A Character from a Novel*, an intimate portrait of Emmanuel Macron during his presidential campaign. His novels have been translated into twenty languages.

MOLLY RINGWALD's writing has appeared in *The New Yorker*, *The New York Times*, *The Guardian*, and *Vogue*, and she is the author of the bestselling novel-in-stories *When It Happens to You*.